WHEN AN OMEGA SNAPS

A LION'S PRIDE #3

EVE LANGLAIS

When An Omega Snaps © 2015 Eve Langlais

Cover Art © Yocla Designs 2015

Produced in Canada

Published by Eve Langlais

http://www.EveLanglais.com

E-ISBN: 978-1927-459-720

Print ISBN: 978-1514382790

This book is a work of fiction and the characters, events and dialogue found within the story are of the author's imagination and are not to be construed as real. Any resemblance to actual events or persons, either living or deceased, is completely coincidental.

No part of this book may be reproduced or shared in any form or by any means, electronic or mechanical, including but not limited to digital copying, file sharing, audio recording, email and printing without permission in writing from the author.

CHAPTER ONE

Leo was just minding his own business when he heard someone shout, "Heads up! Or is that heads down?"

Thunk.

Either way it didn't matter. Leo caught the Frisbee with his noggin, which, given he was in the lobby of the condo complex he lived in, didn't impress him one bit.

Some might have acted on that irritation—gone after the Frisbee tosser and scalped her. Others would have engaged in an unladylike tussle. But as the Pride's omega, he had a certain standard to adhere to. Leo let the irritation roll off his really wide—so wide the college football coach almost cried when he wouldn't play—shoulders.

With a nonchalance and calm that Leo strove to teach others, he kept walking toward the elevator, which happened to be where the purple disc landed. He refrained from crushing it. No need to blame the disc just because its thrower had poor aim.

An unfamiliar scent—feline and delicious— surrounded and brushed past him as a woman skipped by, intent on the Frisbee. The blonde, whom he didn't recognize, stooped over to grab the plastic disc, her cropped athletic shorts molding every curve of her made-for-gripping ass and nibble-worthy thighs.

Everything about her was big, bold, and luscious.

Yummy. And it wasn't just his inner beast that thought so.

Who is this delicious handful? He didn't recall meeting her, and he certainly wouldn't have forgotten her.

The unknown woman straightened and faced him, and by face him, he meant almost eye to eye, which was unheard of given he boasted a height of almost seven feet. Yet this woman with the wicked curves must have stood at least six foot one or a touch more.

She wasn't dainty, not by any stretch, not with the way her impressive breasts strained at her T-shirt, distorting the cartoon on it that said, Delicate Freakn' Flower. Her indented waist was accented by the flare of her hips, the quirk of her lips matched by the mirth in her eyes.

While not a man to allow himself to indulge in strong emotion, Leo was suddenly possessed of a powerful urge to drag this woman into his arms and…do decadent things that would get even his steady heart racing.

"Well, hello there, big fellow. I don't think we've met."

Indeed they hadn't, or he would have remembered her—and remembered to avoid her because anyone could see by the saucy tilt to her hips and the appraising look in her eye that she spelled trouble.

Leo didn't do trouble. He preferred calm moments. Serene outings. Quiet evenings. Very quiet. A quiet she disrupted with her Frisbee antics, so he took her to task. "You're not supposed to play Frisbee inside. It's one of the association rules." He'd know since he helped draft them.

Leo liked rules, and he expected people to follow them. When any group of predators lived in close proximity, keeping hot tempers under control was important, hence his job to enforce the edicts and keep the peace.

"Aw, come on. Are you telling me there's no playing inside either?" Her plump lower lip jutted. "Do you know I got in trouble by a nice policeman for playing on the street? Which was totally unfair. As if it was my fault that guy wasn't paying attention and rear ended someone at the red light."

"You were playing in the road?"

"Road, sidewalk, does it really matter? What's more important is, if I can't play inside, and I can't play outside, where is a girl supposed to play?"

Upstairs, eleventh floor, condo unit 1101. His bedroom had plenty of room. Of course the sport he pictured didn't involve any props. Nor did it include any clothes. But telling her she could play with him naked probably wasn't the answer she looked for. "We don't play in the city. Not enough room. That's what the ranch is for."

"Ah, the farm. That place is still around? Awesome."

"You know of it?" He frowned. While not a closely guarded secret, only those with permission were allowed on the property. Since Leo tended to curate that list, he tended to know anyone who visited. But he couldn't place her. "Who are you? I don't think I've seen you around before."

"Yeah, it's been a while since I visited. That's what happens when a girl gets banned for a few years because of a few silly misunderstandings. Explode one carved pumpkin and people lose their minds. I see the lobby got repainted, no permanent harm done."

Banned? Wait a second. He did know who this lady

was. He'd heard Arik mention something about a cousin on his father's side visiting for a bit. His words were actually, "Damned uncle asked me to let the brat come and hide out for a bit while some kind of calamity blows over in her hometown."

To which Leo replied, "You know you can use the word 'no'. I find it quite effective if I don't want to get embroiled in unsavory situations." The word no helped prevent a lot of unnecessary chaos.

Arik had laughed. "Say no to my uncle? Not happening. You haven't met him yet. He's the one guy I know who would make you look normal sized and when he's not threatening to twist you into a pretzel, he's the nicest guy you ever met. He's also besieged by a set of troublemaking daughters."

Both of whom had been banned by the previous pride alpha for causing too much damage and being a general nuisance.

While she had only recently arrived, Leo could already understand why the old king banished her. "You're that troublemaker from out West, aren't you?"

"Me, a troublemaker?" She fluttered her lashes. The problem was, with a mouth like hers, twisted into a smirk, she failed at the whole innocent look. "No, that's my sister, Teena. I'm Meena, her twin, more commonly known as catastrophe. But you can call me your mate."

With that, she flung herself on him and planted a big, juicy smooch on his lips.

And he liked it.

Rawr.

CHAPTER TWO

Okay, so maybe throwing herself on a stranger and planting a big ol' kiss on his stern lips wasn't the most ladylike thing to do. Then again, Meena had failed her decorum classes—more than once—which drove her mother absolutely mental.

In her defense, she didn't see why a woman needed to learn how to simper, curtsy, or wait for a man to open the door. If it had a handle and her hands weren't full, then why the hell couldn't she open it herself?

Her manners teacher also said nice girls didn't plant smooches on boys. Oh and tell them they were fated mates. That kind of thing tended to freak a guy out.

Freaked or not, he didn't shove her away. As a matter of fact, he let his tongue shove its way into her mouth for a fun and slippery dance. A very short dance that proved quite titillating while it lasted.

"Check it out! Leo's making out with Meena!"

The shouted interruption really deserved a smack, but apparently that wasn't allowed either, at least not with family members, even distantly related ones.

The man she'd laid claim to pulled back slowly as if his lips were reluctant to part from hers. He set her back on her feet, and it belatedly occurred to her that he'd managed to remain standing during the entire affair. How lovely. Not many men could handle her enthusiasm—also known as 'your fat ass', according to her wanted-to-be-punched brother—when she jumped on them. And yes, that was another thing her mother tried to curb, given her enthusiastic habit of flinging herself at people to say hello inadvertently took them to the ground—and on some unfortunate occasions to the emergency room.

Daddy's fault. A big man, he never had a problem catching his twin baby girls, even when they got to be taller than most men.

Lucky her, though, fate had chosen a big hunk of a guy as her mate. Fist pump.

When her man didn't say a word, probably struck speechless by the awesome kiss, she broke the ice. "That was one hot smooch, Pookie. Wanna find somewhere private and make out some more?"

Leo cleared his throat. "I don't think so."

"Oh, would you rather stay here and do it for an audience? It's kind of kinky, but hey, voyeurism, even the reversed kind, is sexy."

Did his eyes cross for a second? "Um, no to that as well. I mean we shouldn't kiss. At all. Anywhere."

"Why not?" She tilted her head as she asked. She wondered at his reluctance. She'd felt his enjoyment pressing against her—hard to miss his impressive size—when she was wrapped around him like a snug Meena coat.

Before he could reply, someone hollered, "Hey Meena, wanna go grab a drink?"

Not really. She kind of wanted to talk more to the big guy, a guy her inner lioness wanted to rub against and lick and do all manner of yummy things to.

Given the stern look he shot her way—and despite the hot kiss—he wasn't inclined to oblige. A shame.

"My crew is calling, and I can see you're just overcome with meeting me. Tell you what. Why don't you take some time to process the fact you've met your future mate—and change the sheets. I will see you later, Pookie." With a waggle of her fingers and a wink, she skipped off and joined her friends, cousins for the most part that she hadn't seen in years.

While she might have been banned for a while by the old alpha, that didn't mean some of the family didn't come out West to visit. Good times that resulted in them getting kicked out of more than one bar.

Lionesses knew how to party.

With the ban lifted, her friends now wanted to show Meena around on their home turf. Finally. Years had gone by since the edict forbidding her from visiting. Meena wasn't in the least disappointed when she heard Arik's dad had retired. The guy was such a strict stick in the mud when it came to silly teenage pranks like putting grease on the lobby floor and turning it into an indoor sliding rink. She'd cleaned it, along with the tree sap on the outdoor wall that they used to play flypaper. And for those who'd never played, it involved running at the wall and splaying yourself to see if you stuck. Like a fly. The person who hung on the wall longest won. Skinny cousin Lolly always emerged victorious.

Linking her arms through those of Zena and Reba, Meena exited the condominium building that housed most of the lion's pride members in this city. Felines, especially lionesses, enjoyed sticking close together, which tended to drive their husbands and boyfriends nuts. But any man brave enough to take on a lioness as a mate had to learn to live with it—or face the stare of dozens of eyes as the women badgered him asking why he thought they should move.

"I can't believe you kissed Leo," exclaimed Zena.

"I loved the expression on his face. Mr. Calm and Stoic looked like he got kicked in the 'nads."

Ouch. That didn't sound pleasant. Nor promising, especially since her conviction he was her soul mate stuck. "Leo? Why does that name sound familiar?" Meena mused aloud.

"Because he's the pride's omega," Reba replied.

"He is? What happened to Tau?"

"Tau retired about two years ago. He tried to stick it out after Arik's daddy finally said screw it and took off for Florida with his lover, Lew, the pride's beta. But Tau and Arik didn't quite see eye to eye, so Arik brought in a whole new crew. You've got Hayder acting as beta and Leo as the omega," explained Reba.

"He's Canadian, which is why he's so calm, on account of those cold winters. It keeps their blood sluggish so they're less prone to outbursts," Zena added.

"What an ignorant thing to say." Reba stopped dead and eyed her best friend. "Canadians are just as hot blooded as any American. Maybe more I think on account of their freakishly cold winters. They need to do something to stay warm. Why, I used to know a French boy from Ontario who could make my panties practically melt off me with just a look."

"Just about any guy who eyeballs you manages to get those suckers off."

"They do not."

"Do too."

Sensing a brawl about to start, and not by her for once, Meena stepped between them, acting as peacemaker.

Would you look at that? My future mate is already having an effect on me.

"Cousins, why don't we agree to disagree?"

"I still say they're all pacifists," Zena said with a smirk.

"With great big dicks and hot tongues."

"The better to broker peace with."

Giggles ensued.

Meena didn't care what nationality he was. "He's cute."

Her statement met with silence and shocked stares.

"What are you looking at me like that for? He is totally cute and super sexy too."

"Are you talking about Leo?"

"Who else? Oh come on, you can't tell me you haven't noticed." How could anyone miss him? Meena had found herself fascinated by him the moment he walked through the glass doors of the lobby. It was why she'd missed her toss on purpose.

Zena wrinkled her nose. "Well, yeah, we noticed he's a stud, but that doesn't mean any of us ever acted on it. Leo's not into dating within the pride. Hell, he barely dates at all, and when he does, he keeps those ladies far away from us. He's kind of shy when it comes to relationships."

"And he tends to stick to human girls. He doesn't like pride girls. Says they're too much trouble," Reba added with a roll of her eyes.

As if Meena would let his usual preference deter her. This Leo fellow was the jam to her peanut butter. The whipped cream to her sundae. The guy to rock her world, break her bed, and maybe help her avoid the disasters that seemed to follow her around, or, at least, manage to calm tempers with his voodoo omega powers when she pissed people off.

In other words, the perfect man.

CHAPTER THREE

What a perfect mess that woman made of his calm mind.

The encounter with Meena had left a taste in Leo's mouth—not a bad one. On the contrary, he could still taste the pink bubblegum flavor. Yummy. Almost as yummy as the feel of her in his arms, all those curves for him to hold. He did so like a woman with meat on her bones.

Just not this woman.

Mate indeed. He snorted again as he walked the few blocks to the steakhouse he liked to frequent. While Leo was a good cook, there were times he enjoyed letting someone else do the work. Especially times like these when his usually calm and orderly emotions were in a rare turmoil.

As Meena bounced off, he watched the waggle of her ass with way more interest than he should have. To his annoyance, his interest was noted and teased upon by the remaining pride ladies lounging in the reception area. He'd not found their ribald and impromptu song entertaining at all. "Leo and Meena sitting in a tree, F-U-C-K-I-

NG." Fighting a blush, he'd bellowed "Behave!" to get them to stop and then glared at them for good measure until they scattered.

But the damage was done. The song spun around in his head. Dammit.

Needing to work off the adrenaline in his body, Leo took the stairs instead of the elevator, pounding the steps, three at a time. By the time he'd reached his floor, without breaking a sweat, or breathing hard, he'd almost managed to temper the urge to stalk her down.

Almost.

His inner feline on the other hand sulked. Mentally giving him the cold shoulder, his inner liger didn't understand why they weren't hunting the female with the incredible scent.

Because we don't go looking for trouble.

Entering his condo, a serene space with a muted color palette—or as Luna called it, "B-o-r-i-n-g."—he kicked off his shoes and made himself a nice cup of green mint tea. And no, it wasn't sissy. Just ask Hayder, who'd made the mistake of taunting him, only to gasp for breath as Leo timed a perfect shot to his diaphragm. As Leo explained to the pride's beta while he recovered, "This tea helps focus the mind, which, in turn, gives me great aim."

Distraction. That was what he needed right now, so he could forget how those plump lips tasted or how Meena's luscious body felt wrapped around him.

Grabbing a hardcover by a favorite author that he'd started a few days previous, he tried to read but couldn't focus. Instead of seeing words, he saw the curve of her lips and the sparkle in her eyes. His cock hardened in remembrance of her heat pressing against him, the hint of her musk surrounding him, begging him to touch and pleasure and…

Despite an urge to throw the book, he placed his bookmark back within its crisp pages and placed it on the table, perfectly aligned with the edge.

Since concentration on written words proved impossible, he resorted to cleaning, but everything in his place was spotless. Yes, he was a compulsive neat freak. At the moment, the only dirty thing around was his mind. Oh, the things he wanted to do to that vexing woman.

But wouldn't.

Focus.

The lotus position comprised of legs crossed, elbows on his knees, eyes closed while emitting a low hum didn't help him to regain his serenity. With all his usual tricks failing, he resorted to the one that never failed.

Food.

Hence why he found himself outside, just as twilight fell, on his way to the best steakhouse in the city. Owned by the pride of course. Lions knew their meat. Looking for a steak, cooked rare with just the right hint of seasoning, a dribble of red-wine-reduced sauce, a double baked stuffed potato, and a side order of sautéed vegetables drizzled in butter sauce? Then get your ass to A Lion's Pride.

His liger, usually a calm fellow, couldn't help a mental twitch of his tail. But it had less to do with the idea of food than the fact that his nose caught a hint of a scent. A certain bubblegum, womanly, oh-shit-she's-here scent.

Luckily the place was huge, and Leo wasn't a coward. He wouldn't run. Chances were this Meena girl had forgotten him by now. And if she hadn't, he'd set her straight—and by straight he didn't mean to his room.

The maître' d smiled when he saw him. "Leo, how nice

of you to join us. Shall I have the kitchen prepare your usual?"

"Yes, please."

"Unfortunately, your preferred table is currently occupied. Actually the entire dining side is fully booked. But I do have a booth on the bar side that will accord you some privacy." How well Othiel knew him.

The leather-wrapped booth was tucked against the wall and high backed. It didn't prevent the noise from flowing over him, but he tolerated it. The low-pitched hum of many voices interspersed with laughter meant people were getting along and having a good time.

No need to omega their asses into behaving.

Not that he'd resort to his *voice*, not in public especially, or around humans. The world wasn't quite ready to discover furry shifters lived and worked among them.

Many of his kind had worried that, with the advent of digital cameras and social media, their secret would become harder to keep.

Wrong.

Social media, special effects, and a need to prove things wrong meant it was easier than ever to explain away strange wild animal sightings in urban areas. Saw a lion walking down the alley? It was some guy on his way to a costume party. Someone uploaded a video of a pair of wolves battling it out in the parking lot of a twenty-four-hour burger joint on a full moon? Obviously a prank animation created by a teen with too much time and computer power at his hands.

Hiding in plain sight had never been easier, but some, like Leo, preferred to stay away from crowds or large gatherings. He had his reasons. Ostracized at a young age by his peers because he was a hybrid—a liger, half-lion, half-tiger—led to him being somewhat shy. It didn't help that he proved an easy target to pick on. Back then, he was but a puny boy with a mother who advocated talking it out. Yeah, talking didn't work well against fists so he often came home with black eyes and loose teeth.

When he hit his teenage years and went through a massive growth spurt, he suddenly found that those who'd once taunted him were now quite eager to engage in discourse instead of fisticuffs. But since Leo knew some of them were hard of hearing, and even more inept at understanding, he sometimes reinforced his oral lessons on proper manners with a well-aimed fist or two.

Spare the fist, raise a rude shifter. Or so his grandma used to say.

When he graduated high school—with honors of course—he left home and attended university, where he met Arik and Hayder. Despite his desire for quiet, the pair seemed determined to drag him along and embroil him in their messes.

To his surprise he enjoyed mediating their dilemmas and, more astonishing, despite their chaotic nature, enjoyed their company. With them, he felt at home. Accepted.

After university, they went their separate ways, Arik to work for the pride's export business along with Hayder while Leo enrolled for a time with a private company specializing in security. Some might have called his work with them mercenary. Others spying. He called it experience and a paycheck. But he didn't love it enough to stay when Arik asked him to join his pride and act as their official omega. An omega's role was as peacemaker in the pride. He was supposed to be the voice of reason, the mediator, the calm one. The one everyone dumped their shit on and demanded help fixing.

He almost said no. Surrounded twenty-four-seven by people, in the city? He was all set to reject the offer when Arik insisted he come meet the pride. The entire clan was gathering for a wedding, a great time for him to meet and get a feel for the folks Arik presided over.

Except Leo never made it to the wedding reception. He made it as far as the hall outside the giant ballroom, where tiny sniffles led him to a little boy, a lion by scent, hiding in a utility closet.

Upon opening the door, he'd dropped to his haunches to bring himself eye level with the quivering lad.

"What's wrong?" For some reason, while adults eyed Leo askance because of his size, women and children always took to him.

This child was no different. "Rory and Callum took my tablet."

And judging by his slight frame, the young boy didn't think he could get it back.

It brought back memories of a time when Leo had to fend for himself against bullies, in a pride where the omega couldn't be bothered to mediate for children, especially not a half-breed one.

In that moment, Leo made up his mind. Here, he could make a difference. He could provide resolution for those needing an advocate, rules to keep the peace, and eat steak any damned day he liked. Yeah, Arik bribed him by taking him to A Lion's Pride and promising he'd always have a free meal if he would only agree to stay.

Throw in a condo and Leo had never left.

He also made Arik regret his decision to give him free food. Leo had a healthy appetite. He took total advantage, but while he didn't have to pay, he did tip well, though, so the staff loved him.

Nursing a tall glass of milk—a liter-sized beer stein since Leo took his health seriously—he closed his eyes and leaned his head back, inhaling the mouth-watering scents of food cooking.

His head snapped as a decadent aroma plopped itself down across from him.

"Pookie! I knew you'd come find me." Meena beamed at him from across the table.

His cock tried to wave hello, but he jammed a fist down on his lap. "I came for dinner."

"Dinner? Oooh. I do so love a man who likes to *eat*." She winked.

He fought a blush. Him. A blush. What the hell? "Shouldn't you return to your friends?" Before he did something crazy like invite her back to his place for dessert.

"They can wait while I have dinner with my Pookie. I mean, I wouldn't want to be rude on our first date."

"This is not a date."

"And yet, there's you, me, and food!" She clapped as she exclaimed the last word, probably because the server arrived bearing a massive platter laden with a ridiculously large steak and all the fixings.

Before he'd finished saying thank you to Claude for being so prompt with his meal, she'd sawed off a piece of his porterhouse and popped it in her mouth. As she chewed, eyes closed, she made happy noises.

Noises that should not be allowed in public.

Noise she should make only while he touched her.

Noises that made him snap, "Do you mind? This is my supper."

"Sorry, Pookie. That was so rude of me. Here, have a bite." The next piece of steak she cut she offered on the tines of her fork, a fork that had touched her lips.

Refuse. We don't share. We—

He devoured it, the bite an absolute delight. Juicy, a slight hint of salt and garlic, butter-soft to chew. His turn to sigh. "Damn, that's good."

"Make that noise again," she growled.

He glanced at her and noticed she stared at his mouth, avidly. Hungrily…

It was both flattering and disturbing. He needed to stop this. Right now. "If you don't mind, I would prefer to eat alone."

"Alone?"

"Yes, alone. While I am complimented by your interest in me, I'm afraid you're mistaken about everything else. We are not on a date. We are not mates. We are nothing. Zilch. Nada." No point in sugarcoating it. Best to lay it all out now before she got any further with this crazy idea they belonged together.

But we do belong to her.

Leo ignored his inner feline as he waited for her outburst. Women never took rejection well. Either they resorted to tears and wailing, or they resorted to screaming and ranting.

But honesty was best.

However, Meena didn't react as expected. Her lips stretched into a full grin, her eyes sparkled, and she leaned forward—pressing her breasts together, causing her neckline to droop and give him a peek at the shadowy valley they created. "Resistance is futile. But cute. Think of me later when you're masturbating, I know I'll be thinking of you."

With a last stolen bite of his dinner, she popped up from her seat and sashayed to the bar.

Don't look. Don't look.

Pfft. He was a cat. Of course he looked, and admired the hypnotic swish of her ass.

She'd taken his rejection a lot better than expected, even if her method was complete denial. However, he appreciated her not making a scene and allowing him to finish his meal in peace, a peace shattered as he enjoyed a hot cocoa with his dessert.

"Do it! Do it!" The raucous laughter from the bar, followed by some shrill shrieks, cut through the gentle buzz of the crowd.

Used to loud women by now—the pride ladies not exactly the quietest sort—he ignored the din as he savored the creamy caramel decadence drizzled atop the moist brownie.

The noise at the bar grew louder. He abstained from craning to see the source, even though his liger kept urging him to take a peek.

Why look when he already knew who hung out at the bar? Despite not peeking, Leo could sense *her* in a way that disturbed him. Surely her earlier proclamation that they were mates was false. Fate wouldn't have paired him with someone so utterly unsuited to his lifestyle and taste.

Okay, maybe she was to his taste because, physically, there was nothing wrong with her. No, his problem lay more with the fact that she personified utter chaos. *I can't imagine spending the rest of my life dealing with turmoil*, even if handling situations—and handling her curves—was something he would totally enjoy.

Finished with the last bite of his meal, he planned to

leave—*Escape now while you can!*—when the noise level rose another notch.

Stay out of it. Don't look. Argh. He couldn't stop himself. Without conscious volition—or because of his sly liger's influence—he glanced over at the sea of mostly blonde heads. As one they chanted, "Chug. Chug. Chug." The lionesses did like their martinis and cocktails, and A Lion's Pride catered to their taste. This place was more than just a steakhouse. The bar boasted knowledgeable bartenders who could make a mean drink for those who liked more than just a beer or wine.

Did it surprise him to note Meena was the center of attention, downing a large cocktail without taking a breath? Such a useful skill to have when swallowing.

Bad kitty.

When she finished her impressive chug, she deposited the glass on the bar and licked her lips.

Moist. Succulent. Lips.

Mmm.

He meant to turn away, but as if sensing his interest, she turned her head and caught his stare. Winked. She also smirked.

Uh-oh. He knew that look. It spelled run.

Alas, he proved too slow.

Bracing her hands on the bar, Meena hoisted herself and stood on the polished surface. She still wore those ridiculously short shorts. Given her position atop the bar, now every man in the place could see how her outfit molded her hourglass curves.

It brought a growl and rising hackles to his inner feline. If only he had a long coat to cover her up. An odd thought given many of the lionesses wore the same outfit or worse and he didn't give a damn.

"Who's going to do some shots with me?"

Hands shot up along with too many voices yelling, "Me!"

Meena beamed. "Awesome. Bartender. A round of tequila for me and my friends."

Tequila never appeared sexier than in that moment because of Miss-Determined-To-Vex-Him.

First, she licked the salt she sprinkled on her hand. Her lithe, pink tongue traced the salty crystals, slowly, languorously.

Would she take that kind of time with naked skin?

Focus. Focus!

He didn't avert his gaze in time. With her head tossed back, her hair tumbling over her shoulders and down her spine to tickle the top of her ass, Meena sucked the tequila from the glass.

I wonder if she likes her hair tugged. Especially if he took her from behind, the soft lushness of her buttocks welcoming his thrusts.

Leo couldn't help but groan.

As for her, she laughed as she took the lemon wedge in her mouth and chomped. Her face contorted, and her lips pursed after she spat the yellow chunk out. "Argh! Woo!" Fist pump.

Utterly insane. Kind of like the rest of the lionesses he knew.

A sane man would escape now. A wise man would run. But he couldn't leave.

As pride omega, it behooved him to ensure things didn't get too out of hand. He wouldn't step in and stop the drinking—that would involve way too much pissing and moaning about him ruining their fun. Then there was the whole annoyance that, when he used his voice of reason on drunken pride ladies, they tended to start calling him big daddy—and presented their bottoms with offers to spank them.

Despite the fact that he might have to drag a few ladies home when alcohol skewed their sense of direction, he'd let the lionesses drink their faces off and then lecture them later on the behavior befitting a young lady. They wouldn't listen, would probably actually laugh, but he'd try. Because that was what omegas did. They provided guidance—and the nagging voice that said "I told you so."

In Meena's case, though, I don't think a verbal lashing will do the trick.

Depended on which part he lashed with his tongue. Too easily could he picture himself between her creamy thighs.

Bad. So bad.

Yummy. So yummy.

He should focus on the speech he'd give the wild lionesses. Or he could skip the useless yapping and put them over his knee like they kept asking. More like put Meena over his knee. Present for punishment those barely covered cheeks in those indecent shorts. Smack his hand on the rounded contour. Lean in to—

"Another round, bartender. B52's this time."

This wouldn't be good.

Now it should be noted, while shapeshifters had heightened metabolisms and could process alcohol quicker than humans, it still had an effect, especially if drunk in copious amounts.

It didn't take a brilliant mind to see the coming catastrophe, especially as the buxom Meena wavered on the bar's polished countertop, her cheeks flushed, her eyes glassy, and her laughter rich and unabashed.

What she didn't have was common sense. Even though she tottered, she kept tossing back the drinks the cheering crowd offered.

"Who wants a blowjob?" she asked.

Me!

On some visceral level, he knew she meant the alcohol shot, but it didn't stop his dick from perking with interest.

Nor did it stop him from imagining her on her knees, eyes peering at him as her cheeks hollowed while her mouth opened wide over his shaft and slid back and forth.

Groan.

Placing his linen napkin on the table, Leo rose, and while he meant to leave—screw sticking around waiting for trouble—he, instead, found himself sauntering in her direction.

A crowd of lionesses stood in his way. It took only a few nudges to get bodies to part before him. For those that didn't get the hint, he grabbed and moved them aside.

As he hit the area around the bar, he didn't say a word. He simply held out his arms, just in time too, to catch a tipsy armful as gravity finally took its toll.

Drunk or not, Meena recognized him. A wide smile stretched her full lips, and a dimple appeared in her cheek. "Hello there, Pookie. I knew you couldn't resist me."

"Did no one ever tell you to not stand on bars?"

"Well, yes, my friend Gina did, but mostly because last time I was wearing a skirt and her boyfriend wouldn't stop peeking up it. She totally started that fight too. As if I wanted her scrawny boyfriend. I prefer a big man. Like you."

The compliment worked. Warmth rushed through him, energizing his nerves, his skin. Everything. It made him hyper aware of her presence in his arms. It also unfortunately was noticed by those around them.

"Nice catch, Leo."

"I won twenty bucks."

"Which is bullshit," grumbled another female voice. "She technically fell off the bar."

"But she didn't hit the floor. You totally owe me."

The lionesses were not deterred at all by the demise of one. On the contrary, a new lioness took her place on top of the bar—funny how Leo wasn't worried about her falling.

He turned to leave and was confronted by Reba who held up a shot in each hand. "Leo and Meena sitting in a tree. K. I. S. S. I. N. G."

Well at least they were singing the more appropriate public version. Ignoring their offer to drink with them, Leo left and waded through the people and tables, aiming for the front door.

Meena didn't seem perturbed at all that he took her away. On the contrary, she giggled. "And he carried her off into the sunset, or in this case moonlight, and they lived happily ever after." Meena scissored her feet, the edge of her toes catching a tray of empty dishes and sending it tipping.

The resulting crash didn't slow his steps. In his mind, the faster he got her out of here, the less chance for more disaster.

And the faster we're alone.

The insidious reminder almost made him stumble.

He set her, and his mind, straight. "My rescue of your demise at the hands of gravity changes nothing. I was simply doing my job as omega. I saw a catastrophe in the making and headed it off." Sounded plausible, if only the pesky truth about his capture of her falling hot body wasn't because he couldn't help himself.

"I don't know if I'd call this a catastrophe. I mean you caught me, and didn't drop me. Nothing got broken, you don't need an ambulance, and now I'm getting carried princess-style by someone not related to me. That is totally awesome, as is the fact I'm close enough to you to do this." This being nibble on his neck amidst catcalls and lewd suggestions from behind them at the bar, which faded in volume and variety as he carried her outside into the fresh air.

The cooler night air didn't stop her hot nips and sucks at his neck. Nor did it cool his ardor, which insisted on tenting his trousers.

Were this any other woman, Leo might have allowed himself to enjoy the caresses. But this was Arik's cousin. This was a woman spoken of in a hushed tone by Hayder —who sported a panicked look whenever her name came up in conjunction with hair. This chaotic female was held in awe by the pride ladies, who said her antics were the stuff of legend.

With that kind of reputation following her, Leo should steer clear.

No. This is our woman. Kiss her back.

His inner beast didn't care about the reasons why they shouldn't enjoy what she offered. Good thing it was the man in control.

While Meena might prove an armful, Leo didn't mind carrying her. It was probably safer for society at large if he did. This way he could ensure she made it back to the condo and to bed before she initiated any disasters.

Did his reluctance to let her go have to do with his enjoyment of her neck nibbling?

Never. He would never stoop to such a thing.

Would he?

He tried to distract himself from the antics of her mouth by talking. "Didn't your mother ever teach you to not drink like a sailor in public?"

"My mother is an uptight prude whose idea of a good time involves needlepoint and making homemade jam. I prefer to live a little. And, besides, where was the harm? I was having a good time. I paid for the drinks up front. I didn't throw up on anyone. I'd say things were going fine."

"You fell off the bar."

"Did I? Or did I notice a certain hunky man approach and decide to test his reflexes?"

"You did not purposely fall."

"If you say so, Pookie." She punctuated her assent with a suck of the skin on his neck.

"Why do you persist in calling me Pookie? My name is Leo."

"Leo is what everyone else calls you. I want my own special name. I choose Pookie. Do you like it? I think the nickname suits you because you're just so big and cuddly."

Appalled, he gaped at her. "I am not cuddly." On the contrary, he preferred to watch movies alone, in his chair.

She snuggled her cheek against his shoulder. "You are totally cuddly. And cute. You also have a great butt."

He did? And no, he did not allow his chest to swell at her praise. "I think you're drunk."

"I might be a little tipsy, but I'm not blind. You are hot. Even if you weren't my mate, I'd totally go after your sweet ass."

"We are not mates."

"Yet."

"Ever." And was it him, or did this conversation have a déjà vu feel to it?

"Playing hard to get. I like it."

"I am not playing. I mean it. I'm not interested in pursuing a relationship."

"Whatever. *Pookie.*" She said it with a mocking inflection before returning to her exploration of his neck.

Deciding that arguing wasn't achieving a thing, he kept walking.

And no he didn't put her down. Don't ask him why. He just didn't. Couldn't.

Because she's ours.

Rawr.

He kept his roar of frustration to himself and ignored the curious gazes that followed his path as he entered the condo and strode straight to an elevator.

Someone cleared their throat, but before they could speak, he growled. "Not a word. Not. One. Single. Word. For those who feel a need to know," felines being curious creatures, "I am putting our inebriated guest to bed."

Meena released her latch on his skin long enough to shout, "Do not disturb! I'm getting lucky tonight."

He closed his eyes and sighed.

Titters followed, cut off only because the elevator doors slid shut behind them. "Was that really necessary?" No hiding his exasperation. And did she look suitably chastened by his glare?

Nope. Not one bit.

An impish tilt to her lips rendered her peek at him utterly adorable. He fought her allure with a stern mien.

"Don't be grumpy, Pookie."

He was not grumpy. He was being patiently stoic. Big

difference. "You insinuated we would be sleeping together."

"Aren't we?" Again, she tried an innocent flutter of lashes.

"No."

Her turn to sigh. "A shame. But I won't take it back. A girl's got her reputation to maintain. Besides, I told Reba and Zena I'd get you into my bed."

"You did what?"

She rolled her eyes. "Oh, don't tell me you have a rule against wagers too."

"I do when they involve me."

"But half of it involves me, so doesn't that mean it's allowed?"

"No."

"Oh, come on. It's not like I wagered anything bad. Just that you'd end up in bed. With me."

"Prepare to lose since I am putting you to bed, not joining you."

"Are you sure? I mean I know it's not really big, being only a queen, but we could snuggle."

Snuggle? If he ended up in bed with her, he'd do more than that. Way more.

As the elevator door slid open, it occurred to him that, with her condo door only feet away, he could set her down and let her make the rest of the way to her bed.

Stupid body still wasn't obeying. *Best to ensure she makes it.* Given her reputation, he wouldn't put it past her to bolt back into trouble the moment he turned his back.

With that kind of reasoning, he had no problem keeping a tight grip on her as he strode the short hall to the door to her place. He knew which suite she occupied, the one reserved for guests. As pride omega, he could open the door by placing his hand on the security panel set in the wall.

In he strode, not paying the décor any mind. He'd seen this place many times before as it hosted visitors to the pride. He also knew exactly where the bedroom was, and he quickly entered it, and finally his arms obeyed, dumping her on the mattress.

She squealed as she bounced, arms and legs splaying—which in those shorts proved practically X-rated.

A true gentleman would have looked away. Apparently, Leo wasn't as obedient to his manners as he liked to think.

But at least one question was answered.

She's wearing panties. Cotton pink ones.

Drool. So sexy.

Some guys might go for the lacy thong type undergarments, but Leo was more turned on by a woman who hid her assets in plain gear. The plainness only served to enhance the natural beauty of a woman's body.

As if Meena needed any more garnishing. He already lusted after her way more than was appropriate.

Help her win the bet. Join her in bed. How sneaky the whisper. Even worse, he couldn't tell if it was his sly feline trying to get him to claim the vexing woman or his own mind trying to get him to cave to temptation.

Not happening.

He pivoted to leave, only to stop when she said, "Where are you going? If you're going to put me to bed properly, shouldn't you at least strip me?"

Ten. Nine. Eight. He didn't calm down until zero. Actually, he still wasn't calm, but he turned around anyhow, against his better judgment, unable to control the actions of his body.

There she lay, still splayed on her back, arms folded under her head. Her pose pulled up her shirt so that a strip of skin peeked between the hem of her top and her shorts. As for her shorts, damn, they did look uncomfortably snug. She really should remove them—along with her surely confining bra.

I'll bet those breasts could use a massage after being bound all day.

He tucked his hands behind his back. "I am not stripping you. You can do that yourself."

While we watch. His inner feline approved of that plan, even if it knew that wasn't Leo's intent.

She obviously thought it was. "A voyeur. How sexy. Prepare yourself to be wowed by my uber sexy moves."

He was wowed, and he also fought hard to not laugh—and pounce on her to ravish.

Laughter because those tiny jean shorts were determined to stay on.

"Stupid gigantic steak for dinner and killer cheesecake for dessert," she grumbled as she squirmed and struggled with her bottoms.

"When did you eat?" Because she'd had only a few bites of his.

"Before you got there. Which is why I let you keep yours. I wasn't really hungry. But I am now." Her wink turned into a squint as she stuck her tongue out, arched her back, and tugged at her jeans, which had rolled into a fabric wad around her hips and stuck.

"Need a hand?" he asked. Not because he truly wanted to touch her—he did, he totally did—but because he couldn't stand watching her thrust and roll her hips anymore. It made a man want to pin her to the bed and have her gyrate that lower body with erotic purpose.

"About time you offered." She stilled and grinned at him, unabashed and inviting.

Leaning down, he didn't waste time, just grabbed the fabric hugging each hip and pulled.

Rip. The denim shredded and released her from its prison. Without it, though, she was revealed.

What had he said about plain panties enhancing? Never more true than now.

Pink cotton molded her lower pelvis and couldn't hide the moisture soaking the thin strip of fabric covering her sex. The undergarment might hide her mound, but it couldn't stem the musk of her arousal.

She wants me.

I want her.

Must have her.

Take her.

Claim her.

Help!

Leo succumbed to something he'd not felt in years. Panic.

"I think you can handle it from here." By herself. Without him. No more touching. No more being a helpful guy and helping her strip.

"But what about my bra?" She cupped heavy breasts and shot him a sultry, pleading look.

Free the beauties!

He took a step forward. Caught himself.

Must escape. He didn't walk. He ran! Took off as if a herd of stampeding elephants was after him, ready to squish him. And before anyone laughed, stampeding elephants were no joking matter. He should know. He'd barely survived one of their mad dashes.

Just like he barely escaped her apartment unscathed.

I should have never gone in there. I should have walked her to the door and left.

He knew this, and yet, he couldn't help himself.

Couldn't help but want her.

It was enough to make even his temperature boil—with arousal.

Entering his own place, he immediately went to the bathroom and turned the shower on. Cold water only. He could lie and say he was conserving energy by abstaining from the hot, but his motive was to calm the raging heat within him.

The icy chill of the shower did help ease some of his erection, but it couldn't wipe his mind clean of her.

Unbidden, but welcome, he gripped himself, the thickness of his cock a testament to her effect on him. He wrapped his fingers around it, closed his eyes, and let the fantasy take over.

Perhaps by letting it play out, he'd diminish its power over him.

So he let himself imagine she knelt before him. Glorious and naked. Her golden hair streaming about her shoulders and kissing the top of her splendid breasts. What did her nipples look like? He'd left before finding out, but he imagined they were large, succulent, just like the rest of her.

And she would be an enthusiastic lover. On her knees, she'd grip him tight. Oh yes. Snug hand stroking his cock back and forth, rubbing the soft skin, providing friction. A quick lick to the tip, a gentle caress that would turn into a full-on lap of his mushroom head.

Groan.

A suck into the warmth of her mouth, a mouth that would suction and bathe him in moist heat.

Sigh.

As she sucked him, her hand would work him, back and forth, back and forth, faster, faster. His hips thrust, plunged, pushed his cock deeper. What kind of sounds would she make? Appreciative moans. Maybe she would indulge in a few nips of his flesh, hard enough to make him gasp.

"Take me, Leo. Take me now," she'd sweetly beg.

Would he bend her over to claim her or finish in her mouth? She would sense his dilemma and whisper, *"Come for me. Let me taste you."*

Holy fuck.

He climaxed. Hot spurts of cream washed down the drain. Relief at last.

Now, perhaps, he could manage to resist her strange allure. Obviously, he'd gone much too long without release. A man needed to come on a regular basis if he wanted to control his baser urges.

No wonder he'd almost succumbed to the vexing woman. He was just overdue.

Yet, if that was the case, then why did the thought of her winking and whispering, *"Can we do it again?"* lift his spent cock?

I can't be horny again. Not so soon.

Yet he was, and the more he tried to not think about her, the more he couldn't help remembering the taste of her on his lips, the feel of her nibbling on his neck.

Argh. His bout of masturbation hadn't worked. What was wrong with him?

Since his body seemed determined to return to its feverish state, he made a point of staying in the frigid stream, head bowed, breathing and focusing on mundane matters. The upcoming pride picnic at the farm. The newest baby girl born in the pride, whose shocking red hair had them all wondering what genetic throwback she'd prove to be when she hit her teens.

When he felt he'd regained control of himself, he finally stepped from the shower and wrapped a towel around his loins. Given the lack of heat during his polar plunge, no mist obscured his mirror, and thus did a blotch of unexpected color catch his attention. He turned and took a closer peek.

"I don't fucking believe it. She marked me." Indeed she had. A nicely purpled hickey stood out in stark contrast to the rest of his neck.

She marked us!

It irritated—pleased—him. It also wouldn't last long. He healed rather quickly.

He touched his fingers to the mark, reliving for a moment the act that put it there. The tender touch of her lips, the sensual heat of her breath, the shocking arousal and need to taste her skin.

Sigh.

Back into the cold shower he went.

CHAPTER FOUR

Dark lashes feathered against cheeks. Full lips appeared soft and inviting. Dark hair, mussed instead of perfectly brushed.

No lines of annoyance to mar his face. She enjoyed it while she could. Chances were it wouldn't last much longer. Especially since she was about to rouse him.

"Wakey, wakey, Pookie."

To his credit, Leo didn't scream. Not like Hayder did the last time Meena perched on him and woke him with a stare. At the time, she was only twelve, a lot smaller, oh and she was wearing a bogeyman mask. Still, the yelp he let loose, totally un-lion like. From time to time, she enjoyed calling his voicemail and playing the sound clip for giggles.

Leo didn't let out anything but a grunt when he opened an eye and noted her straddling his impressively wide chest.

Unlike her brother, Barry, he didn't fling her off. Unlike her daddy, he didn't tell her to go bother her mother. And unlike her last boyfriend, he didn't gasp for air and demand an ambulance. What a pussy her ex turned out to be, letting a few cracked ribs get in the way of good-morning sex.

Leo did none of those things. He closed his eyes and went back to sleep.

Hunh. Did he perhaps not notice her sitting there?

She wiggled. Kind of hard to miss her squishing him, wasn't it?

He didn't budge.

Down she leaned until her face only hovered an inch or so above his. He didn't open his eyes but he did ask, in a tone of voice she well knew—exasperation with a touch of resignation—"How did you get in here?"

"Through the door, of course."

"It was locked."

"I know. A good thing I got a key."

"How the hell did you get a key? The door is handprint coded. Nobody has a key."

"Does the how really matter? As your mate, I needed access to our place."

"This is not our place. This is my condo."

"Yes, I can tell." She wrinkled her nose. "This place is like some immaculate and boring showroom. Don't worry. I've got plans to redecorate."

"I like my decor as is."

"I'm sure you do, but since we'll be sharing it as mates—"

"We're not mated," he growled in a sexy tone she really enjoyed.

"Yet." Spoken with absolute conviction. Meena was a strong believer in fate.

"Ever." He sounded so convinced.

How cute. "Have I told you that I love a challenge?"

"This is not a game."

"You're right. It's not. A courtship doesn't have losers, only winners."

He sighed. Again, another sound she was all too familiar with.

"What do you want?"

Wasn't it obvious? "You."

"Other than me."

"World peace."

He snorted. "Not happening."

"Shoes I can buy off the rack instead of special order." Size twelve feet for a woman presented challenges.

"Go barefoot, it's better for you. What else?"

"Scorching-hot sex."

That made his eyes shoot open. He stared at her, and she smiled, especially as a certain part of him went from semi-erect to full-on steel pole, a thick and long one. How nice to discover he was proportioned.

"We are not having sex."

"Are you sure about that?" She squirmed atop him, the thrill of the rub sending frissons through her body.

"Very."

"If you're not in the mood, then what is this?" She did a slow grind against the proof of his arousal.

His eyes turned a deep shade of smoky blue, a sign of his passion. A sign he was about to break loose. A sign he—

"That, Vex, is called an urge to pee. It's a natural male bodily reaction that occurs upon waking."

His response didn't deflate her one bit. She thought it cute he was lying to her and playing hard to get. No one wanted to mate with a manwhore.

Still though, it didn't mean she let him off the hook.

She gave him another rub, which she immensely enjoyed. "A shame. I do so love a little morning nookie. It helps get the day going." While he made no outward sound, she did notice a teeny tiny tic by his left eye, and even he couldn't fully hide the tension in his body.

Done torturing him for the moment—pleasant as it proved—she rolled off his delightful body onto his bed. "Go. Pee. I'll wait for you," she announced when he didn't immediately move.

"I can't."

"Why not? Are you the type who gets stage fright if he thinks someone is listening to him pee?"

"No. But I am kind of not dressed for company. So if you wouldn't mind…"

"Mind what? Getting a look at the merchandise?" She smiled as she laced her hands behind her head. "Go ahead and flaunt it, Pookie. I can't wait to see what you've got."

Ooh, look at that. The tic got a little bit more pronounced.

"I am not going to parade naked in front of you. It wouldn't be proper."

"Now you sound like my mother. Put some clothes on. Wear a bathing suit when you swim. Don't flash your boobs for beads. This isn't New Orleans."

That was definitely another sigh. "I am starting to see why you were banned from visiting."

"Hey, it wasn't my fault the mice got out. They were supposed to be a surprise. How was I to know they'd get in the wiring?"

"Dare I ask why you had mice?"

"To play a game of course."

"What game involves live rodents?"

She rolled her eyes. "Like duh. Mousetrap of course."

"Of course." Even he couldn't stop the twitch of his lips. "Interesting as this conversation is, I am going to the washroom. I expect you to be gone when I return."

"Or else?"

"What do you mean or else? I've given you an order, and as a guest of the pride, you will obey."

"Sure thing, Pookie."

"And stop calling me Pookie."

"Would you prefer Snookums?"

"No!"

She might have laughed at his harried tone if he'd not chosen that moment to fling the covers back, revealing lots of flesh. Muscled, slightly tanned, delectable flesh.

Wanna nibble.

While her cat might want a bite, Meena wanted to pounce on him. Especially since the bold man, while initially shy about showing off, didn't move in a hurried fashion to the bathroom.

Nope. He rolled off the bed, presented her with an ass —in serious need of teeth marks, hers of course—then moved with a sensual grace that had her sighing.

Oh what a fine-looking male.

Mine. The possessive thought took her a bit by surprise. Meena usually shared everything with everyone.

Until now. Now the idea of another woman eyeballing her man made Meena a teensy tiny bit upset—upset as in, I'll-rip-her-eyes-out-if-she-stares-too-long. At least now she understood why Grandma had spent a year in jail. Some things were worth doing time for.

"Have a good pee," she shouted. "And don't worry at all about the fact I can hear you. A healthy bladder is a good thing. It means we don't need to budget for diapers."

The bathroom door shut, and the fan went on—which

made her giggle. Despite his order to leave, she didn't move. She flopped her arms out on the bed, a nice big bed.

She felt quite at home in it, and she greatly enjoyed Leo's scent, a masculine aroma that she inhaled with every breath.

Leo might still be fighting his attraction to her, but he'd come around. She'd make sure of it.

Comfortable and a little tired—the darned man had left her aching the previous night and that, in turn, led to a lack of sleep—she napped, only to wake some time later to his grumbled, "You're still here?"

She stretched as she opened her eyes, and despite his grumpy query, she noted he watched her every movement.

He wasn't the only one watching. She took in his appearance that included him being freshly showered, shaved, and unfortunately dressed in khakis and a T-shirt. What a shame. She wouldn't have minded a peek at the front of him to see if it presented as splendidly as the rear.

"You look positively yummy, Pookie."

"Don't change the subject. I thought I told you to leave."

She gave him an honest answer. "You did, but I didn't think you really meant it, so I stayed. Besides, I don't want to go."

Nope. She was staying right here.

But by right here, she meant on his bed and not on the floor where he dumped her!

CHAPTER FIVE

So perhaps lifting his mattress and sending Meena tumbling to the floor wasn't the calmest decision, or the nicest, but dammit, Leo had to do something.

Bad enough when he'd woken with her perched atop him. Smelling so delicious. Feeling so delectable. Tempting him to roll her onto her back and give her the morning sex they both craved.

The darned woman was right about one thing. He did want her. Craved her bad.

He'd lied about having to pee. He lied about a lot of things it seemed since he'd met her. The biggest was the one where he kept telling himself he didn't want her.

I want her. Want her too bloody much.

Hence why he tipped her off the bed. It was that or pounce on the delectable Meena and kiss her chattering lips, plunge his erection between her plump and perfect thighs, and lose himself in the splendor she promised.

Madness.

He needed to focus, and to do that, he needed to rid himself of temptation. Despite the urge to offer her a hand to help her off the floor, he turned—ignoring the voice in his head that screamed, "Where are your manners?"—and, instead, headed for his kitchen. In that direction he'd score a much-needed morning coffee. Then again, was that really the brightest choice? Perhaps he should keep his nerves caffeine free, especially around her.

He didn't quite make it to his destination. A body tackled him from behind and yelled, "Gotcha!"

Taken off guard, he staggered but soon regained his footing, even as Meena's legs wrapped around him and her arms looped around his shoulders.

"What the hell are you doing, Vex?"

"Vex? Is that your nickname for me?"

"Yes, because you seemed determined to vex me to death."

Any other woman would have probably taken offense. Hit him possibly too. The one clinging to his back with anaconda strength? "I like it. It's cute. So when are you getting it tattooed with a heart on your body?"

How the hell did her mind work? "I don't do tattoos."

"I don't blame you. Your body is already an awesome work of art. How about I get one instead? Right on my left ass cheek, maybe something that looks like a brand. Property of Leo. Or how about Pookie's Delight?"

Yes and yes. "No! No tattoos. At all."

"Spoilsport."

He didn't reply, just continued his journey to the kitchen, with one determined lioness on his back.

"So what's for breakfast?" she asked.

Her, on the counter, with a drizzle of syrup that needed licking from the plump breasts pressing against his back. "If I say nothing, will you leave?"

"Nope. But if you don't get us some food, then I'll be

forced to cook, and I'm going to tell you right now, you really, really don't want me to do that," she confided in a low whisper. "The last time the firemen came to the house, they said the only thing I was allowed to cook from here on out was cereal with milk."

Nothing could have stopped his chuckle. "Well then, I guess you'd better leave if you're expecting sustenance."

"I'm sure I could find something else to eat." She practically purred the words in his ear.

Surely that unmanly "eep" didn't come from him?

It took him only a second to slip his shoes on, grab his wallet, and snare her shoes by the door before he had them both in the elevator. She slid down his back, but given her height, she could still whisper hotly in his ear, "You do know that the longer you fight it, the more explosive it's going to be. Foreplay, Pookie. This whole denial thing is like a long, extended foreplay session. And when you finally can't say no anymore, watch out. I am going to make you see stars."

Stars. Fireworks. More like the inside of a jail cell because, if he wasn't careful, he would end up taking her in public and getting arrested for an indecent act.

Some of his ardor managed to cool when they entered the lobby. Hard to maintain an erection when a half-dozen pair of eyes fixed on him and Meena.

Speculative looks bounced between them. If he were a callow youth, he might have blushed as they came to the wrong assumption. If he were Hayder, he would have strutted with feigned prowess. Leo settled for something between a scowl and placid disinterest. He disliked rumors, especially ones about him.

Meena had no such shame. Smiling wide, she strutted to the group. "Morning, peeps. Isn't it a beautiful day?"

She didn't say anything untoward. She didn't have to. The implication was blatant—if false.

Since she seemed distracted, he used that moment to escape. It failed.

He had no sooner hit the sidewalk than she was bouncing alongside him. "So where are you taking me to breakfast?"

"I'm not. I'm going to a coffee house to grab a Danish." A half-dozen with about three of their breakfast wraps and a large banana smoothie.

"Ooh, are those the ones with the icing? Can I lick yours?" She batted her lashes at him innocently. The dare in her eyes was anything but.

He didn't reply. He didn't have to. The brat already knew how she affected him.

Just before they reached the coffee shop, her cell phone rang. Peeking at the display caused a frown to crease her brow.

What, finally something to mar her happy mien? He wondered what it was—so he could get rid of it. He didn't like her less than smiling.

Whoa. Where did that thought come from? Whatever perturbed her had nothing to do with him. *Don't care. None of my business.* His curious cat could keep its speculations to itself.

Leaving her on the sidewalk, he entered the coffee shop. After ordering his usual, plus a few extra—because she looked like the type to ask for a bite—he turned and leaned against a pillar. If he wanted to lie, he'd claim he did it so the staff wouldn't get nervous. Not everyone could handle a guy his size keeping an eye on them. Except the folks here knew him and weren't intimidated one bit. So why did he really stare out the window?

Because a certain lioness still stood there and a part of him couldn't help but keep an eye and wonder what mischief she planned.

Through the coffee shop's large plate glass window, he saw her pacing on the sidewalk, her face a study in animation as she talked, one arm tucked to her side holding the phone to her ear, the other flailing and gesticulating.

What a dilemma she presented. She seemed determined to drive him insane—with lust. On a mission to muddle his emotions—with her quirky personality. On a path to change his future—with determination.

She was also being accosted!

Rawr.

CHAPTER SIX

"Get in the car." The unmistakable Russian accent had Meena rolling her eyes.

"I gotta go, Teena." Hanging up on her sister, Meena turned and took in the sight of the long black sedan, a Lincoln Town Car, of course, because Dmitri liked to travel in style. "I am not getting in, Dmitri."

The crack of space afforded by the tinted window wasn't enough for her to see his handsome mug, but she could imagine it, dark-haired, blue-eyed, and arrogant beyond belief. Wouldn't it figure her reason for leaving home would show up?

"How did you find me?"

"I am a man of many resources, as you should know."

Yeah, she knew, which was why when she ran out on him she caught the first plane ride back from Russia. Once home, she figured she could expect a few calls demanding her return. What she didn't expect was for him to follow.

Dmitri was also very old-school in that, apparently, no wasn't an answer. Not one a woman could use at any rate. And in case anyone thought there was a certain irony in her thinking Leo's no's were playing hard to get while hers were emphatic, it should be noted Leo was her mate. Dmitri was a vacation fling, one that had never even made it to the bedroom.

Totally different.

With Leo, she had sparks. Tingles. With Dmitri, meh, he was cute, but he didn't make her heart race like a certain liger.

"You need to let me go, Dmitri, and move on. I am not going to marry you."

"I will have you." Such conviction, and he'd brought some muscle to try and prove his statement. A pair of brutes exited the car. Dmitri's order of, "Don't hurt her," made her tsk aloud.

Please. If he thought to subdue her, he should have brought more guys. As the one gorilla—and seriously, despite his obvious humanity, she had to wonder at his ancestry—grabbed for her arm, she sidestepped, causing him to snare only air. She, on the other hand, didn't miss.

Her foot swung out and cracked goon number one in the knee. He let out a yelp of pain, but before she could take him out fully, the second guy lunged for her. She ducked under his grasping hands and thrust, her fist connecting with his diaphragm. He gasped for breath. She took no mercy and kneed him in the groin, just as goon number one made his next move.

With a tinkle of bells, the door to the coffee shop opened, and a very calm-sounding Leo said, "Lay a finger on her, and I will rip your arm off and beat you with it."

As threats went, it was adorable. Especially since, given his size and mien, Leo probably could.

The idiot didn't listen. The thug went to grab Meena's

arm, and curiosity made her let him instead of breaking his fingers.

Why exert herself when Pookie seemed determined to come to her rescue?

While outwardly he appeared cool and composed, a wild storm brewed in his eyes as Leo growled, "I said don't touch."

Crack. Yup. There was one guy who wouldn't be touching anything with that arm for a while, and he'd probably end up hoarse with the way he was screaming.

Pussy.

In the distance, sirens wailed to life, and it didn't take Dmitri's barked, "Get in the car, you idiots," for the thugs to realize their attempt at a coerced kidnapping had failed.

Meena didn't bother watching the car speed off, not when she had something much more important to attend to. Like a man who thought she needed saving. How her dad would laugh when he heard about it. Her sister, Teena, would sigh about how romantic it was. Her mom, on the other hand, would chastise Meena for causing chaos once again.

Turning to Leo, who wore a formidable glower, she threw herself at him. Apparently, he half expected it because his arms opened wide, and he caught her—without even a tiny stagger!

She latched her legs around his waist, draped her arms around his neck, and exclaimed, "Pookie, you were awesome. You saved me from those big, bad men. You're like a knight in Under Armour." Not entirely true. He wore a plain black Fruit of the Loom T-shirt. But she could totally picture him in one of those form-fitting tees that Under Armour specialized in that would mold his perfect chest.

On second thought, given how it would show off his impressive musculature, perhaps she should leave his wardrobe alone. No use taunting the female public with what they couldn't have. It would also mean less blood for her to rinse if they dared to touch.

"I'd hardly say I saved you. You seemed to be doing all right on your own."

She planted a big smooch on his lips and declared him, "My hero."

Most men might have puffed in pride at being compared to a hero—or sank to the ground crushed under her weight. Leo just stood there, frowning at her and then off into the distance where the car had fled.

"Who were those guys?"

"Oh, those were just Dmitri's men."

"And who is Dmitri?"

"The guy I was supposed to marry."

CHAPTER SEVEN

Of all the answers Leo expected, that wasn't one of them.

A pimp looking for vulnerable girls, it happened more often than it should.

An organ seller on the prowl for healthy organs also possible, especially since he'd actually come across it in the past—before he put an end to it. In an ironic twist, the seller saved five lives with his healthy offerings. Good thing he had his donor card signed.

Even a recruiter for the underground shifter fights would have made more sense than Meena's reply.

"He's your fiancé?" he blurted out. Just the very word fiancé had his body tensing, his liger growling, and his temperature rising.

"Not exactly."

Tension built behind his brow as he anticipated a convoluted explanation. "Is he, or isn't he?"

"Can't we eat first? I'm *starving*." She purred the word and stared at his lips. It was enough to make him want to roar. Instead, one hand cupping her lovely butt, he opened the door to the coffee shop and went to the counter, where Joe raised a brow, but he didn't say anything. As a shifter, Joe knew better, of course, than to get involved. Each member of his staff was shifter related as well, and on purpose, given their proximity to the condominium complex housing a fair number of the pride.

As a bear, Joe tended to keep to himself. He managed the coffee shop with his family, which was comprised of three daughters, all married, and a wife. He wasn't just their local baker and coffee maker. He also knew the value of discretion, but Leo still had to ask.

"Did anyone call the cops?" In other words, should he and Meena skedaddle before some uniforms appeared asking questions?

Joe shook his head just as the police car, with its wailing sirens, screamed past, on route to another crime.

"Here's your order, Leo," Rosalie announced, plopping the big bag of goodies on the counter, along with a pair of yellow and creamy-looking smoothies.

"That smells so good," Meena murmured against his ear. She also nipped it before she slid down his body, and by slide he meant he felt every inch of her curvy frame rub against him.

Joe inclined his head in her direction, silently asking, *Who is she?*

"Joe and Rosalie, meet Vex, also known as Meena. She's visiting the pride for a while."

A giggle left Meena as she tucked against him, wrapping an arm around his waist. "More than visiting. Pookie and I are engaged to be mated. So you'll be seeing a lot more of me."

There went that tic again. He heard Joe's snicker. He

saw Rosalie's wide smile. He sensed the jaws of the trap surrounding him, ready to snap shut.

But he didn't run. He couldn't. She wouldn't let go even when he gestured for Meena to grab her drink.

Before she did, she peeked into the bag of goodies. "Ooh. Aah. Yummy. Are we eating it here or taking it home, Pookie?"

By home, he assumed she meant his place, which boasted privacy and a bed. Since the type of eating that reasoning evoked had nothing to do with actual food, he chose the table farthest from the door.

He plopped the bag of breakfast treats on the table along with his drink before sinking onto a seat that squeaked alarmingly.

Seated across from him, Meena pursed her lips and sucked from the straw, the hollow in her cheeks distracting but not enough for him to forget what had just happened.

A fiancé? It wasn't just his curious cat with questions. The man wanted to know what the hell as well.

But it took two Danishes and one breakfast wrap—stuffed with fluffy eggs, bacon, green peppers and sharp cheddar—before she would deign to reply to any of his queries.

As she licked her lips—the tip of her pink tongue a tempting tease—he launched his interrogation. "Exactly who were those guys, and why were they trying to force you into that car?"

"Those were Dmitri's goons, and like I said, they were trying to get me to go with them so that Dmitri could haul my butt in front of a priest and have him marry us."

"By your use of haul, I am going to assume you're not keen on marrying the guy."

Her nose wrinkled, and she shook her head. "Nope. I've been trying to avoid him."

The pieces of part of the puzzle fell into place. "This Dmitri fellow is why you're here, isn't he? That's why Arik let you come back. You're hiding."

"Me, hide? Of course not. My parents just thought it was time I came for a visit now that Arik's in charge." Once again, she failed the whole guileless thing.

"Thought or insisted?"

Her lips jutted in a pout, the lower succulent lip begging for a nibble. He refrained. "Talk."

"Fine. They banished me. It was deemed best if I laid low and out of sight for a while, given the problems I incurred whilst in Russia."

"You were in Russia? Doing what?"

"Flower hunting."

He blinked. "Flower hunting? Is that even a thing?"

"Well, yeah. Rare seeds fetch a pretty price, as do hybrids of select species. My mom runs a very successful flower shop, and part of the reason she's in such high demand is because I travel for her and snag interesting seeds and samples."

"So help me out here, how does flower picking get you in trouble?"

"Well, as it turns out, the blooms I was seeking, the *Symplocarpus renifolius*, were in a garden."

"A public garden?"

"Not exactly. More like a private one. Which really is kind of rude given how rare they are. Flowers should be shared."

He leaned back in his seat, ignored the ominous groan of metal, and prepared for a convoluted story. And yeah, he knew Meena well enough by now that he could think this with certainty. "So you knocked on this guy or gal's door and asked to see them?"

She squirmed in her seat and took a second to suck a long pull from her straw. Cheeks in. Lips pursed. Excellent suction.

He tore his gaze away. "Did you trespass?"

"Kind of. But I didn't mean to. I just wanted to see if they were there before I bothered anyone. So I kind of climbed the big stone wall he had running around the place."

"It didn't occur to you that he had the wall to keep people out?"

"Well, once I encountered the barbed wire, I did, but by then, I was curious."

The failing of many a feline, a need to see what hid on the other side. Not a failing Leo suffered. He usually was tall enough to note the other side had the same color grass.

"So you hopped the fence. You snuck into the garden—"

"After giving some cute Rottweilers that came to say hello some belly rubs."

The pulse behind his forehead intensified. "You do realize they could have torn you to pieces?"

Again, she fluttered her lashes in an innocent look he didn't buy for a moment. "Why would they do that? I give really good rubs. Want me to prove it?"

Yes! "No."

"You're right. Now isn't the time. We should wait until we're back home so I can *rub* you properly."

No point in correcting her that rubs would not happen. *Why not?*

His liger really didn't understand why he was so

adamant about keeping her at arm's length—especially since up close felt so much better.

Keep the conversation—and mind—on track. He wondered if it was a ploy on her part to distract him from what he really wanted to know. Judging by the way her foot tried to inch its way up his leg, probably. He trapped the sneaky foot between his knees. He needed the rest of the story, especially the part where she wound up engaged to a Russian fiancé. "So you evaded all the security measures, found the rare flower thingies, got caught and arrested." Had she been blackmailed by a police officer or government official into agreeing to marriage in order to avoid charges? Green card marriages happened all the time.

"Not exactly. I did get caught. Dmitri saw me on camera and came out in person to ask me what I was doing. When I told him I needed his flowers, he said he'd give me one if we went on a date. He proposed that night."

"Hold on. A guy catches you trespassing in his garden and looking to steal some rare flower, and then he takes you to dinner and asks you to marry him?"

She nodded.

"And you said yes?"

"Of course not. I'm not easy. Besides, while handsome—"

He couldn't help but growl at the compliment.

"Dmitri never really got my kitten purring."

"Lions don't purr."

"I wasn't talking about that pussy." She smirked, probably because her frank correction had him squirming.

Good to know she wasn't attracted to the guy, but it still didn't explain the biggest question. "If you weren't interested in him, then how the hell did you end up engaged?"

"Oh, did I forget to mention Dmitri is head of the shifter mob in Russia? After my third refusal, he locked me up and went ahead with plans for the wedding anyhow."

"Except the wedding didn't happen. You are still single." *Not for long.* His liger had very definite ideas of the future.

"Single and a good thing too otherwise I might have never met you and we wouldn't be about to plan our future together. And don't worry, even if Dmitri had managed to slide a ring on my finger, once I met my true mate, which is you, I'm sure between me and daddy, we could have arranged for a divorce or an accident. But, fate was on my side. I'm all yours, Pookie." She beamed at him.

Bang. That was the sound his head made as it hit the table. *Bang. Bang. Bang.*

"Pookie, what are you doing? Is this some kind of seizure? Do you need me to put something in your mouth so you don't choke?"

He was suffering from some kind of malaise all right. He rested his head on the table, eyes closed, trying to find the serenity that had fled the moment he met her. "How did you escape if he had you locked up?" Because that information might come in handy if he ever needed to corral her so he could get a head start.

"Let's just say I pulled a Houdini slash runaway bride. Like literally. I escaped the day before the wedding using my mad climbing skills. Since his place is out in like the middle of nowhere, I hotwired this sweet crotch rocket he had sitting out front."

He raised a brow.

"Okay, so I didn't twist any wires. I used the key. But, you do realize that sounds way less exciting."

"Only you would think that."

"Why thank you, Pookie, you already understand me so well. Anyhow, I drove like my daddy was chasing me, which he did a few times when I was a teenager and I snuck out of the house, and made it to the airport. I stowed away on a plane, which looks a lot more fun in the movies by the way, and made it back home. Most guys would have stopped at that point but Dmitri, being stubborn, called a few times spouting off, so I had my number changed."

"But?"

"But, he got my family's number and started calling them. Which was fine. My aunts and stuff blocked him, but thing is, he showed up on my parents' doorstep while I was out shopping. My parents are vacationing in Mexico, and so Aunt Cecily had to deal with him."

"They scared her."

She laughed. "Scare my Aunt Cecily? Not in this lifetime. She wields a mean right hook. Daddy's sister is the one who taught me to fight dirty."

"Something had to have happened to get you banished."

"Well, she was kind of worried about me, on account of me being delicate and stuff."

He couldn't help but snort.

"Yeah, that was my reaction too, but that's what I get for being the youngest in the family. Teena beat me into the world by like ten seconds. Anyhow, Aunt Cecily would have kept me around, except the goons trampled Mama's flower garden during one of their kidnapping attempts."

"You got banished over flowers?"

"No, I got banished before the goons did any more damage to Mama's stuff. When my mother cries, Daddy gets a little upset, and when Daddy gets upset, things happen. Dealing with the disposal of bodies is always a pain, and law enforcement really frowns upon murder. And Daddy's been trying so hard to stay out of jail. Anyhow, for the good of the family, it was strongly suggested I take an extended vacation in the hopes my absence would see Dmitri call off his paid thugs and give up on the whole marriage business."

"Except he realized you took off and followed you here."

A frown creased her brow. "Yeah, which is weird because I was certain I didn't have a tail."

"Well, you're going to have one now, twenty-four-seven, until I locate this Dmitri fellow and tell him to get the hell out of pride territory."

"You'd do that for me?" She shot him a pleased smile.

"I'd do that for anyone being forced to marry an ass who can't take no for an answer."

Most women would have shown disappointment at being lumped into a generic group. Not her. She smiled even wider. "Pookie, you are a true hero, saving damsels in distress. You are going to make such a good husband."

Not if he pulled a runaway groom.

"I really feel like I should clarify your misassumption about our relationship. As in, we don't have one. Will never have one. Will never happen."

Ha. The derisive snort didn't come from Meena. His liger was the one who found his claims amusing.

So did Meena. "Oh, Pookie, you are so adorable when you're being stern. It makes me want to dive across this table, throw myself in your lap, and plant the biggest smooch on you."

The threat had him bracing for impact—and his dick hardening in anticipation.

Alas, for once, she didn't act.

"Unlucky for you, given the last time I tried that, I collapsed the table, and my lunch companion flipped backward in his chair and ended up in the hospital with a concussion, I'll refrain."

"I would have caught you." Surely that wasn't him encouraging her?

A wicked smile curved her lips. "I know you would have. A man like you knows how to handle a girl like me."

He'd handle her with both his hands, on her naked flesh. So much gorgeous skin to caress and—

"Pookie," she whispered, "you're rumbling again, and while it is super sexy, a few non-felines have just walked in."

He snapped back to the present, once again utterly distracted by the woman before him. "We should head back. I've got things to do."

"Things? Ooh. That sounds utterly decadent. What kind of things are you planning? I'm very partial to nipple play just so you know."

The bag with its leftover treats provided a shield to hide the tenting of his trousers, but nothing could quell the heat in his blood.

Why did she do things on purpose to tease him?

Why are we not taking her up on her offer?

Why wouldn't his liger go take a fucking nap like other bloody felines?

A glower didn't deter her from linking her arm through his as they left. A tight-lipped countenance didn't stem her adorable chattering as they walked. A firm leash on his emotions didn't prevent the spurt of pleasure at her touch. A denial of their involvement didn't stop his growl of jealousy when some yuppies they passed on the sidewalk swiveled to give her a second look.

Were the teeth he bared necessary?

Yes.

Was the sigh as he entered the lobby and a dozen lionesses went "ooh" avoidable? No. Nor could he avoid the snickers that followed Luna singing, "Bow-chica-wow-wow," especially since Meena joined in and began the impromptu dance that involved a lot of hip shaking and breast jiggling.

Throw her over our shoulder and take her to our room. We must claim her before another does.

What happened to his usually staid and laid back inner feline?

The right woman happened.

But what was right for his wild side wasn't what the more serious man side wanted.

She is chaos.

Yes. And wondrous for it.

She is physically perfect.

And tempting him to take a bite.

She'll never let you have a moment of peace.

His life would have purpose.

She would love me with the passion and embrace of a hurricane.

But could he survive the storm?

Or should he try and outrun it?

She would catch us. She is strong. A true huntress.

Rawr.

Possible life-changing inner conversations were best

conducted out of sight, especially since it made him less mindful of his surroundings allowing his cousin Luna to sidle alongside and mutter, "I see the look in your eye."

"What look?"

"The one that sees something yummy it wants to eat."

Was he truly that obvious? "I'm not hungry. I just had breakfast."

Luna elbowed him as she snickered. "Way to pretend ignorance. I know that you know what I know is happening."

"Say that fast five times."

She did. Luna wasn't just quick on her feet.

"So when are you claiming her?" the nosy woman asked.

"Never."

He ignored his feline collapsing in a heap.

"Leo. I am shocked at you. Aren't you the one who advocates honesty?"

"Only if it won't cause irreparable harm. Then even giant white lies are allowed. Anything to hold back the insidious forces of chaos."

"I can't believe you'd reject her on account of her history of causing catastrophes. Sure, shit happens around Meena, like microwaves blowing up on account of the aluminum foil holding the quiche she tried to cook for lunch. But that kitchen needed remodeling anyhow."

"I'm the pride's omega."

"And?"

"It is up to me to keep peace in the pride."

"So who better to take Meena as his woman than you? You'll be like the Meena whisperer. And she'll be the tequila shot to get your blood pumping."

"Are you implying I'm boring?"

"Sometimes. You gotta admit you can be pretty uptight. I mean whenever there's a good brawl nowadays, you're right in there knocking heads together. Tossing someone at a wall. Totally bringing the peace in like record time. It's so annoying. No one's allowed to have any fun anymore."

Except him. He didn't so much interfere because the minor skirmishes needed stopping but more because boredom meant he needed to do something.

"So your theory is I should take Vex as a mate"—he pointed at Meena, where she currently twerked against a potted palm tree—"to get the stick out of my ass?"

"Nah, keep the stick. Being uptight is part of being you, but spend a little less time constantly worrying about us and do something for yourself."

Do Meena. Yeah. His liger wholeheartedly agreed with Luna.

But Leo ruled his body—and his heart.

"Meena is simply a guest, one who will stay here for a short time before flitting off." Leaving him.

He didn't like that thought at all.

Sad meow.

CHAPTER EIGHT

Judging by the glower on Leo's face, he was thinking again. Really, the man did use that smart noggin of his way too much. He thought too much. Worried too much. Didn't lose control enough.

It made her wonder just how wild he'd get when he finally snapped. And he would. A man that tightly sprung couldn't hold on to his control forever. Beneath that placid and grumpy exterior lurked a beast of a man, one with hot blood and untamed passion.

That man would scratch. *Rawr*.

If she could ever figure out how to free him from his cage of denial.

Noting he had turned away and was striding to the elevators, without her, she stopped getting fresh with the plant and skipped after him.

"Oh, Pookie, where are you going?"

"To work."

"Can I *come*?" On his tongue or shaft. Either would do. She tossed him a saucy wink and look. There went that tic by his eye again.

"No."

"You are such a tease, Pookie."

"And you're intentionally vexing me."

"Gotta live up to my nickname."

The elevator door slid open, and he stepped inside. To her surprise, he held the door when it would have shut. "What are you waiting for? Get in."

"I thought you said I couldn't come."

"You can't," he said, reaching out to draw her in. "But it occurs to me, given the incident at the coffee bar, that I should escort you to your condo and strongly advise you to remain there."

"You want me to stay inside?" She wrinkled her nose. "That doesn't sound like much fun."

"Neither would waking up married to a mobster."

"What are you talking about? I'd have plenty of fun. Of course, the staff might not like the mess I make. Cold water only goes so far with stains." She shot him a ferocious smile that should have had him shaking a stern finger advocating peaceful resolutions. A more optimistic part of her hoped he'd snare her close, plant a kiss on her lips, and tell her she wouldn't have to kill the Russian. Leo would do it himself if he dared lay a finger on her.

With them both in the elevator cab, Leo allowed the doors to seal shut and hit the number for her floor. As soon as the elevator lurched, he eyed her and said, "I'm afraid to ask what you're thinking."

"Screw telling. Let me show you." Meena made her move.

Against the wall she shoved him. Her lower pelvis ground against him, and she planted a hot kiss on his lips.

He didn't shove her away. He didn't cry out in pain, complaining she was crushing him. He kissed her back.

At least for a moment. Just when she ventured to touch the seam of his lips with the tip of her tongue, he turned his head.

"**Stop!**"

Oh the cheater. He used his mighty omega voice against her. Commanding. Trying to dominate. It sent a tingle through her, and her lips throbbed, poised so close to him.

"Are you trying to control me?" she murmured, the heat of her breath moist against his skin.

"If I have to. You can't just throw yourself at me."

"You were the one who said you'd catch me."

"This isn't what I meant. I don't want this."

She undulated her lower body against him. "Liar."

"Vex…"

The warning tone just made her smile. "We've reached my floor. Escort me to my door, you know, to make sure I don't cause any catastrophes."

"If I don't, what will you do?"

She let a broad smile answer.

He sighed and exited the elevator.

So far her plan to seduce Leo after breakfast, in that fabulously huge bed of his, didn't seem fated to happen. Even outright propositioning wasn't working!

Time to step things up a notch. With about twenty feet to go, she made a stab at holding his hand.

Quicker than she could blink, he stuffed his hand in the pocket of his pants.

Such a sly liger. As if his ploy would stop her. With his hands tucked away, it left him vulnerable for—

Smack!

"What the hell was that for?" He couldn't hide the shock in his tone.

"Flaunt a nice butt and expect it to get slapped." Hey, she took her pleasure where she could.

"I am not flaunting anything."

She rolled her eyes. "Pookie, I know it's not your fault. A man with your level of sexy just can't help affecting women. Just keep in mind it will be your fault, though, when I get in trouble for kicking the asses of the bitches admiring your assets." Because where he was concerned, she might have an itsy-bitsy possessive streak.

A tic, tight lips, and a rumble. Given how coiled Leo seemed, she couldn't help comparing him to a Jack in a box. Wind it, wind it, wind it, *POP!*

But the pop wouldn't happen today. As soon as they reached the door of her complimentary—and very temporary—condo, he ditched her with a firm admonition to, "Stay put."

She managed not to snicker. Obedience wasn't her strong suit.

"Where are you going?" she asked.

"To work."

"Have a good day, Pookie. I'll miss you." Given the strut of his ass in those pants, she uttered a strident whistle. "Damn, that's a fine view."

He didn't miss a beat, but she could have sworn his shoulders widened. "Behave!" was his last uttered order before he entered the elevator.

Behave? And miss all the fun?

He'd no sooner left than she flounced down the hall to the door marked in red letters, Exit. The stairwell provided a quick way to skip down to the main floor. Once she hit the lobby level, with a wave at her peeps hanging, she strode without pause out the glass doors.

Direct defiance. Maybe Leo would punish her.

She had a skirt short enough to work should he decide to put her over his knee for some correction.

Down to the sidewalk she skipped, heading toward where she spotted Dmitri's dark sedan idling by the curb across the road. While she'd not seen him following, it didn't surprise her that he knew where she was staying. A man with his money and connections wouldn't have a problem getting information.

A good thing he followed, too, because it made her getting in touch with Dmitri a lot easier. Even Leo couldn't get too mad. It wasn't as if she went far. So she was almost listening, right?

Ignoring the traffic—which honked in appreciation of her flounce—she crossed the road and approached the rear passenger window. It lowered at her approach.

Leaning with her arms crossed against the sill, she glanced in and noted Dmitri seated alone on the seat, impeccably attired in a suit and tie. The man didn't know the meaning of the word casual.

His lips stretched into a welcoming smile. "Meena, *lyubov moya,* have you come to your senses?"

Odd how his Russian endearment, which translated to my love, didn't come across as cute as Leo's nickname of Vex.

"Why are you stalking me?"

"Is it stalking given we're engaged?"

Stubborn tiger. "I'm not marrying you, Dmitri."

"But we had a deal."

"Holding me hostage isn't a deal. And besides, as it turns out, we can't be together."

"Why ever not?"

"Because I've met my mate."

One dark brow arched. "Do not tell me you believe in

that superstition about fated mates and other such nonsense."

"Yes, I do. So you see, pursuing me is pointless. I've met my match."

His eyes narrowed. "You say you've met him, and yet, you are not claimed."

Minor detail. "Yet."

"The mating fever can still be broken. I could take you right now and have you on a plane to Russia, having a priest conduct the ceremony and claiming another rank in the Mile High Club within the hour."

Dmitri, the owner of a private jet, was still miffed she ranked higher than him when it came to airplane antics. She'd dated a pilot for a while. Saw the world. Then got banned from a certain airline for accidentally causing a cargo plane to crash. In her defense, she dared anyone not to react a little violently if they got a charley horse while in the throes of an orgasm. She now refrained from strenuous activity in moving vehicles.

"I wouldn't advise trying to force me into anything."

A familiar haughty expression tilted his chin. "I don't take advice from women."

"You should. Especially if you don't want your ass kicked by one." It wasn't Meena that threatened but Luna who shoved in alongside her. It didn't surprise her Luna appeared. The girl had a knack for sniffing out possible catastrophes and making sure she got a piece of the action.

"I will not be threatened." Dmitri was a king when it came to imperial decrees. A pity no one here would listen.

"Who said it was a threat?" Luna grinned. "Think of it more as a promise. See, this is America, dude, and we don't take kindly to misogynists who think they can coerce a woman into matrimony."

"What she said," Meena added. "I already tossed one burning bra into some guy's car. Don't make me do it again." Because apparently that would cause a girl to lose insurance coverage, for like ever.

"Don't you dare harm my rental."

"You rented this?" Luna stuck her head in farther, taking a peek around. She let out a low whistle. "I have to say, this is a nice car. Although, I personally prefer a Lexus to a Lincoln."

"Lexus is for boys. I am a man."

Luna snickered. "A man who can't convince a girl to marry him and has to resort to kidnapping."

Dmitri glared. Luna smirked while Meena caught a glimmer for a moment of why perhaps some people thought she should be avoided.

I guess maybe I do have a touch of unpredictability surrounding me. But in this case, she could get rid of it in a grown-up fashion. "I think you should leave. Now." Before anyone needed stitches and ice packs.

"I am not leaving, *lyubov moya*. I will have you. Willing or not."

Meena couldn't help but roll her eyes. Would Dmitri never get it? "Is your English really that bad? What part of you can't have me do you not grasp? I am tired of dealing with you. Since you refuse to believe I'm off the market, why don't you take it up with my fiancé?"

"Fiancé?" Luna hissed. "When did you get engaged, and does Leo know?"

"Of course he knows. Kind of. Okay, not really, but he'll come around."

"You're engaged to Leo?" Funny how high an incredulous note could pitch.

"Not yet, but I will be. Soon. It's just a matter of time.

So that means I'm off the market." She fixed Dmitri with a stare. "If you want to talk to my man about it, then come to Jungle Beat tonight. Me and my Pookie will be waiting."

"Leo doesn't dance," Luna muttered in a low tone.

"He will." She'd make sure of it.

CHAPTER NINE

Leo's plan to make sure that Russian mobster left Meena alone wasn't going well.

"What do you mean we can't go after the guy?"

Seated behind his massive mahogany desk, Arik spared Leo a glance. "Because he's a diplomat."

"And? So what? He wants to force Meena to marry him."

"Is that really a bad thing?"

Don't roar. Don't roar. Arik didn't mean what he said. Anyone could see Meena getting married to the Russian mobster was a bad idea.

Yeah, because she belongs to me.

He didn't bother arguing with his mental state. He argued instead with his alpha. "Sure Meena might be a tad high spirited—"

"A tad?"

"But that doesn't mean we should condone a forced marriage. We prevented Arabella from getting shackled. Hell, we went to war with the Lycans to protect her."

"That was different. They meant to kill her, and they

were abusive. Dmitri, while somewhat old-fashioned, isn't an asshat. He'll treat her right."

"He's a bloody mobster."

"By necessity. Things are different over in Russia. More untamed. He does what is needed to keep him and his clan safe."

"He's not getting her."

Arik leaned back in his seat and eyed him. "Mind telling me what this is really about? What's your interest in my cousin, anyhow?"

"Nothing. I just don't like seeing any woman accosted."

Snort. "Meena can take care of herself."

"That's not the point. She shouldn't have to."

"Says a guy who has yet to really get to know my cousin. Trust me, a few more days of her special brand of cluster-fucking and you'll be tying her up and delivering her to Dmitri yourself."

Tying her up. Now there was a plan. Thing was his version had her spread eagle on his bed.

It was only when Hayder slapped him on the back and asked him if everything was okay that Leo realized he was banging his head off the wall.

Even with Vex out of sight, she still plagued him. So he wasn't surprised when he received a report that she'd, once again, gone out of her way to cause mischief.

"I gotta go." He no sooner read the text message than he abruptly left. Erratic behavior, but necessary. Omega mission time. Keep one problem-prone lioness from getting into more trouble.

Jogging to his destination would probably prove faster than trying to flag a cab during early afternoon traffic. It also would help work off some of his tension.

Or, in his case, simply ensure he arrived more adrenalized.

Blood pounding, he barged into the boutique. His nostrils flared immediately, catching her scent.

So much for obeying his request she stay inside.

Determined to chastise her, he followed her trail to the back of the store. Before he could bellow for her, Meena flung a curtain back in the change area and beamed his way.

"Pookie! I was hoping you'd show up."

"Hoping? Reba sent me a text message saying you were trying on dresses for your future mate."

"I am. I want to look my best for my Pookie."

No wall to hit, so he slapped his forehead with both hands then gripped it, tugging at his hair. "We are not mates."

"Yet," she sang. "But it's coming. Now, if you're done being adorably contrary, can you give me a hand? I am having problems getting this dress zipped up."

"And you couldn't ask Zena or Reba to help you?"

"Where's the fun in that?" she asked, not at all repentant she'd made him run blocks.

She presented her back to him, a swath of tempting flesh with the strip of her bra crossing it.

Run. Run. Run, you fucking idiot.

Fingers reached for the zipper tab, his fingers, how odd. He tugged and pulled the enclosure shut, resisting the temptation to run a knuckle along the length of her spine.

In the tight space of the change room, her essence surrounded him. She glanced at the mirror that displayed them. Him, not quite overshadowing her, and yet, his hands looked so large, so right, where they rested on her hips.

How the hell did those get there?

Perhaps the same force had moved them as the one that saw him kissing the exposed skin of her neck. How dare she tempt him by pinning her hair atop her head in a sloppy bun?

He dragged his mouth along the creamy flesh, watching in the mirror as her eyes went to half-mast. Her lips parted. Her cheeks took on a rosy flush.

And her nipples…Despite her bra, the silky fabric of the dress outlined them in all their erect splendor.

She couldn't hide the effect he had on her. Then again, knowing her, he knew she wouldn't conceal. She reveled in her attraction to him. Didn't even try to deny the fact that she wanted him.

"I like it when you touch me," she whispered.

And I like it when I touch you. His teeth grazed her skin, just a touch of hard edge but enough to have her shuddering.

"*Leo.*" She just about growled his name, her voice thick with desire, her body taut with need.

"Hey, Meena, I found an even shorter dress for you to try. Well, hey there, Leo. I wasn't expecting you to join us." Damn Reba for interrupting!

As if scalded, he jumped away from Meena, stumbling back from the cubicle. He sought to regain a measure of composure and resorted to habit. Nothing like a good chastisement to draw attention away from his own dilemma. "I told Meena to stay in her condo."

"No, you suggested I stay there. But I had things to do."

"Things like going to talk to your ex after he tried to kidnap you!" He gave her his sternest glare.

"Now, Pookie, don't be jealous. Wait, what am I saying?" She slapped herself in the forehead. "Be jealous. Wildly, ragingly so. Then sweep me into your arms and help me make use of this large enough cubicle."

She flattened herself against the mirror and smiled in a beckoning manner.

He took a step away. *I will not let her bewitch me into playing her game.*

He wouldn't let her seduce him.

Stay strong. Don't give in. If he could stay away from her, then maybe he stood a chance of resisting her allure.

Reba mocked his retreat. "I don't believe it. Leo's afraid of a girl."

Not just any girl. The one who could change the course of his life.

"Behave!" he yelled before turning tail and bolting.

Ha. He showed her. He escaped before she could draw him into her sensual web of madness.

Pussy.

His liger had no respect.

I am doing this for our own good.

Liar.

Problem with having a discussion with yourself was you couldn't hide the real truth.

Truth was he was attracted to her, but…he could fight it if he avoided her.

Problem was she expected his maneuver and planned for it.

The phone call caught him off guard, especially since he'd not given her his number. She also didn't seem like the type to call. He'd kind of expected her to show up at his condo door, a door he'd had a deadbolt installed on so she couldn't barge on in and pounce him.

Instead, his cell phone went off, singing the one and only stalker song, The Police's 'Every Breath You Take'.

Super apt, especially once he realized who called.

How delighted she sounded when he answered with a gruff, "Yeah."

"Pookie!"

"How did you get this number?" And even more baffling, how had she programmed his ring tone? Just how many more mad skills did she possess? *Let's find out.*

"Oh please. As if I wouldn't know your number. I also know your date of birth, favorite sports team, restaurant and meal of choice, as well as the fact you're a fan of the missionary position."

"How the hell did you find all that out?"

"I have my ways. But I don't think you'd like them, so let's just pretend you told me. By the way, if you need to call me, anytime, I'm in your contacts list under M, for mine."

He pinched the bridge of his nose, less out of exasperation with her and more out of annoyance with himself for the spurt of pleasure at her use of mine.

Because she knows she's ours. His liger enjoyed the possessive feeling. Leo, on the other hand, felt another panic attack coming on.

"What do you want, Vex?"

"Didn't we already cover this topic this morning in bed?"

I want you. Yeah, he remembered. "Vex—"

She interrupted before he could finish.

"But I'm not calling about my desire to ravish your delectable male body."

She's not? Surely the sinking sensation wasn't disappointment.

"I'm calling to ask you to go to a club with me tonight. I am in the mood to dance."

"For a girl I told to stay put, you're doing your best to put yourself in harm's way. That Dmitri guy is still out there looking for you. It's not safe."

She snickered. "Not safe for who?"

"A lady shouldn't have to defend herself against a man."

"You and your old-school attitude are so cute. My daddy is going to like you. Or, at the very least, hopefully not punch you like he did my last few boyfriends."

"Why did he punch them?"

"To see if they were tough enough for his baby girl of course." He could practically hear the duh in her reply.

"Did they pass?"

"Would I be single if they had?"

Bet he could take a punch without a stagger. Not that he really cared what Meena's dad thought of him. "It's nice that your daddy is so protective, but he's not here right now. I am, and I'm telling you to stay put and not go out."

"Are you forbidding me?" She laughed. "That is so sexy. And so not happening. I am going out with the girls tonight. The question is, will you come with me?"

Dammit. Did the woman have no sense? Or was she trying to drive him insane?

Too bad. He wasn't playing her game. No club or dancing for him. And he told her so in no uncertain terms. He also played dirty and used his omega voice.

Because I am the one in control here. Not you.
Rawr!

CHAPTER TEN

"No, I will not go with you." Even though they spoke on the phone, she could practically see Leo shake his head. "I don't do clubs, and I most certainly do not dance."

"Well, that totally sucks. I wore a really cute dress just for you. It's short, which means easy access for you. How big are the bathroom stalls at this club?"

The rumble he emitted came through loud and clear. She grinned.

"You're right. Too public. We should probably restrict our public nookie to dark alleys. I can be noisier there."

"Would you stop with the teasing, Vex? I am not going. I don't care how short your skirt is. Just be sure to stick with the group going with you."

"What, no more stern warnings to stay home and out of trouble?"

"Would you listen?"

"No." Mama always said to stick to the truth when dealing with your husband. Even an almost hubby. Unless it was about how much she spent on clothes, then it was grab a delicious catered dinner and tell him you worked all day making it.

"If you're not going to listen, then I'd just be wasting my breath."

"Well, I have to say I am surprised at you, Pookie, and proud that you're already so secure in our relationship. Most men would have a jealous fit knowing their future mate was going to be seeing their ex-fiancé at a dance club, especially in my barely legal skirt. But you're obviously more evolved than most guys and confident in our commitment."

Tick, tock. The clock echoed loudly in the sudden silence that stretched as he absorbed her news.

In a low tone, with a hint of growl, he said, "What did you say? Who's going to be there?"

"Dmitri. Remember how I ran into him today, well, I kind of told him we were an item. But that didn't seem to deter him. I wonder if he's one of those guys who gets off on that cuckold fantasy thing."

"Get to the point, Vex."

"I am. See, when he just wouldn't take no for an answer, I told him to meet us tonight so he could see just how happy we are together."

"We are not together."

"Yeah. I guess that will be kind of obvious at the club tonight. But don't worry, Pookie, even if he tries something, I'll have my girls with me. I'm sure it will be all right."

He bombed her with his omega voice. "**Meena. I forbid you from going.**"

Oops, had she forgotten to mention the voice didn't quite work on her? Doctor's test couldn't figure out why. "Gotta go, Pookie."

She hung up on him and smirked. A little crazy jealousy never hurt anyone. Well, except for the girl in the lobby who admitted she thought Leo had the most dreamy eyes. Meena was sure the black eye wouldn't take too long to heal.

Tucking her cell phone into her purse, she presented a bright smile to Reba, Zena, and Luna, her gal pals for the night, who should try closing their jaws. The gaping look really wasn't attractive. "Ready, ladies?"

The evening was about to get interesting, especially since she could swear she heard a major roar just before she slipped into the cab they'd called.

Awesome. Pookie's coming.

CHAPTER ELEVEN

I can't believe I came. And not in the way he needed.

A sane man would have called in a security detail for the foolish lioness determined to thwart him and put herself in danger. A smart liger would steer clear of the catastrophe in the making known as Meena.

That was another Leo. A Leo not consumed by jealousy. A Leo not burning with a need to protect.

This Leo stalked into the dance club—that he usually avoided like a flea bath after a romp in the woods—his eyes lasering through the bodies in search of one person.

Given her height, made even more extraordinary by those surely-dangerous-for-her-health heels, Meena towered over the club-goers.

Towered and drew the eye.

How glorious she appeared, her blonde hair pinned atop her head with only a few fat golden curls dangling down. She wore a dress that on a shorter girl might have proved decent but, on her, with those long thighs, exposed a lot of leg. It also displayed a lot of bosom as it hugged her breasts, the neckline stretching and drawing attention to the deep shadowy cleft.

Mine.

He wasn't sure if he thought the word or growled it. Either way, when he began to walk toward her, the crowd parted, giving him a path straight to her. Not that she noticed.

Back to him, she shook and shimmied, her boisterous laughter clear to him, even with the pulsing rhythm of the music.

Coming to a stop behind her, he waited for her to acknowledge him.

She continued to dance, ass shaking, arms waving.

He frowned and stared harder. Surely the prickling sensation set off her instincts. Predators always knew when someone eyeballed them. Except either Meena didn't feel it or she ignored it.

Reba, Zena, and Luna, the pride girls she'd chosen to come with, saw him but didn't let on. They did, however, smirk.

Unacceptable. And by that he meant Meena's lack of awareness, of him. He knew when she was in a room. He could smell her in the lobby. The elevator. Even now amidst a crowd of sweating, perfumed bodies, her essence was distinct to him. Surely his scent was a recognizable flavor to her too?

It irked him that she didn't turn around.

A part of him urged him to act, to grab her and march her sexy ass back to the condominium where he could shake her—in private, wearing fewer clothes. Then after he'd shaken her for driving him mental, he'd kiss her for causing him to lose control.

But…as much merit as that plan held, there was something about the hypnotic sway of her hips as she gyrated to the music. Something about her wanton movements that lulled him.

Instead of putting a stop to her hedonistic motions, Leo did something he never did.

Never.

Ever.

He danced.

Less danced than gave in to temptation. His hands palmed her undulating waist, and his body moved in close, close enough to touch hers. His lips hovered over the moist skin of her nape, the musk of her surrounding him in a heady perfume.

He let her body control their movements. Hip thrust left. Booty shake right. His body followed her sinuous pattern, her buttocks fitting perfectly against his groin.

Dancing proved easier, and much more erotic, than he expected. Arousing too.

And did he forget to mention aggravating? Especially when she twirled in his arms, and her eyes widened in surprise. "Pookie, you came."

Who the hell did she think was grinding against her? A bristling liger almost rose to the surface. He definitely scowled with more teeth than was human.

"You didn't give me much of a choice."

She draped her arms around his neck and smiled, easing some of his irritation with the way her body rubbed against his. "I can take care of myself, you know. I'm not a delicate freaking flower in need of a hero. Although"—she leaned in close, her heels giving her the extra inches needed to have her lips at the right height for his—"I am happy you came."

Not as happy as a certain body part of his at her proximity.

"We're not staying. I just came to fetch you."

She whirled in his arms, once again presenting her back, and an ass that rubbed across him most enticingly. "Leave? Already? But I'm having fun."

Technically, so was he. However, it was time Meena learned that the pride had rules. As omega, he enforced them. Rule number one, at least where Meena was concerned, consisted of staying out of trouble. "Fun or not, we are leaving before your ex-beau appears and causes a scene."

She laughed. "Oh, don't worry about that. Dmitri won't do anything in public. He might be a ruthless crime lord, but he knows better than to break the rules for our kind." The rules that stated no shifter, of any caste, would do anything that would bring attention to them. A rule enforced by the High Council, which didn't like to show leniency.

"How can you seriously claim he wouldn't try anything crazy and public? He tried to kidnap you off the street."

"Yes, that was a little naughty of him, I'll admit."

"The next time he tries that, you might not get so lucky. Or do you want to marry the guy after all?"

She whirled to face him, lips pursed. "Pookie, how could you say that? I told you, we're fated to be together."

Leo did something underhanded. Dirty. Or should he call it pleasurable? "If you're so sure of that, then leave with me. Now. Let's go back to my place."

He could see by the shining in her eyes that she thought he'd finally succumbed, that he was about to debauch her and make love to her sweet, voluptuous body.

Aren't we? His inner feline seemed to think they would.

No. This is just so we can get her out of here before—

The cloud of scents in the place was the only reason he didn't sense the guy before some stranger spun Meena away, daring to lay his hands on her and steal her for a dance. A slow tempo one that allowed the stranger to sway against her.

To her credit, Meena didn't appear pleased with the change in partners. She also did nothing to move away. She kept dancing, with another man's hands on her.

Breathe in. Breathe out. Focus on something other than the fact that the interloper's hands lingered a little too close to the curve of her upper butt cheek. Breathe in. Breathe out. Ignore how snugly the other man held Vex against him.

Tear his face off.

He shouldn't. He couldn't. He was in public. She didn't belong to him. He had no excuse for jealousy. No real reason to snap.

Yada. Yada. Leo didn't care.

His blood went into an immediate boil. A red film descended over his eyes, and his liger rose close enough to the surface to emit a less-than-human growl.

Stop touching.

With only three steps, Leo reached the dancing couple and tapped on the black silk-clad shoulder of the usurper.

The stranger, who this close smelled distinctively of tiger, turned his head and, with a brow raised in a supercilious arch, drawled, "Fuck off. The lady is taken."

Oh, she was taken all right. *She's mine. Mine!*

Dammit. Her constant assertions even had him

convinced she belonged to him. But setting that dilemma aside, he concentrated on the current problem.

"You're Dmitri, aren't you?" The accent when the guy spoke, and the exasperation on Meena's face, gave it away.

"I am, and just so you know, before you act, I have the High Council's permission to be in this territory. My business interests have brought me here."

"Business?" Leo sneered, not a familiar shape for his lips. "I don't think dancing counts as business."

"Would you deny a man some *pleasure*?" The Russian prick practically purred the word as he drew Meena closer.

At least she didn't appear happy about Dmitri's appearance. With a sharp elbow, she loosened his grip.

"Would you stop it with the anaconda routine? Just because I didn't break your nose when you ruined my nice dance with Pookie doesn't mean you get to touch. This"—she gestured to her body—"belongs to one man only." With a toss of her head, she flounced to Leo's side. His arm automatically wound around her, possessive. Protective.

Mine.

Oops, he might have said that aloud.

"Yours?" Dmitri lifted a brow. "And yet I see no claiming marks nor a ring, which makes the fair Meena fair game."

"She doesn't want you."

"For the moment. She'll come around." Dmitri didn't seem perturbed at all by her lack of interest in his suit.

"Arik and the rest of the pride won't stand back and let you kidnap her." Although, they wouldn't have much left to punish once Leo got through with this Russian dick.

"Are you sure about that? I did mention to your alpha my intention to make Meena my bride. He said good luck."

"Meena isn't leaving with you."

"And who will stop me from taking her? She is unclaimed, and she gave her word she would marry me. You cannot watch her every second of the day. Eventually, you'll lessen your guard. I will catch her in a weak moment. I will have her bound and gagged and on a plane to Russia, where I know a priest who isn't picky about the words 'I do'. That same night, I will plant my seed, and she will belong to me."

With every word, Leo's ire built. And built. Until he snapped. "I said she's mine!" The declaration shot from him along with his fist.

And a second first happened that night. Calm and collected Leo started a very public and violent fight.

Rawr!

CHAPTER TWELVE

Oh boy, am I ever going to get the blame for this.

Then again, when didn't Meena get blamed when shit happened? Although, maybe in this one instance, she did technically start the fight. She'd thought herself very mature the way she didn't react when Dmitri pussy-blocked her by stealing her from a dirty-dancing Leo. Meena's first impulse was to rake her nails down his face before snagging his long hair, yanking his head down, and repeatedly slamming her knee into his smirking visage.

But Leo deserved a lady and ladies didn't beat the hell out of ex-boyfriends for interrupting a dance. Apparently, new boyfriends had that privilege.

Meena gaped as Leo and Dmitri tussled. She'd not expected things to progress into such a public fight.

She'd predicted the men would have words. However, that was all that should have happened. That was Leo's usual MO—which for those who hadn't dated a cop stood for *modus operandi* or, in simple English, how a suspect perpetrated their crime. But back to Leo and his snap with serenity. She'd spent the better part of the day with the lionesses, picking their brains about her Pookie, and the one thing they all unanimously claimed was he was the most level-headed guy ever.

Sure, he sometimes knocked some heads together or stared at cubs with his rapier gaze until they promised to behave. Yet, it should be noted he did those things to keep the peace, not destroy it. Leo never condoned violence unless there was no other recourse. He was the first one to counsel calm, and counting to ten, or hitting a wall instead of a breakable face.

In this instance, she'd not heard him count. He'd not hit a wall, unless the brick-headed stubbornness of Dmitri's face counted.

Thwack!

"Yay." Yes, that was her cheering for her Pookie aloud. Since it seemed he hadn't heard, she said it louder, yodeled it as a matter of fact. "You get him, Pookie. Show him who's the biggest, baddest pussy around."

Leo turned his head at that, narrowing his blue gaze on her. Totally annoyed. Totally adrenalized. Totally hot. "Vex!" How sexy her nickname sounded when he growled it.

She could tell he totally dug the encouragement. She waggled her fingers at him and meant to say, "You're welcome," but instead shouted, "Behind you!"

During that moment of inattention—which really Leo should have known better than to indulge in—Dmitri threw a mighty hook.

Had she mentioned just how sigh-worthy big her Pookie was? The perfectly aimed blow hit Leo in the jaw, and the force snapped his head to the side. But it certainly didn't fell him. Not even close. On the contrary, the punch brought the predator in him alive.

As he rotated his jaw, Leo's gaze flicked her way, his eyes lit with a wildness, his lip quirked, almost in amusement, and then he acted. His fist retaliated then his elbow, snapping Dmitri in the nose.

Any other man, even shifter, might have quickly succumbed, but the Russian Siberian tiger was more than a match for the hybrid lion/tiger.

Put them in a ring and they'd have brought in a fortune. They certainly put on a good show.

Blood trailed from Dmitri's lip from where Leo's fist struck him. However, that didn't stop the Russian from giving as good as he got. Size-wise, Leo held a slight edge, but what Dmitri lacked in girth, he made up for in skill.

Even if Meena wasn't interested in marrying him, it didn't mean she couldn't admire the grace of Dmitri's movement and his uncanny intuition when it came to dodging blows.

Leo wasn't too shabby either. While he'd obviously not grown up on the mean streets of Russia, he knew how to throw a punch, wrestle a man, and look totally hot in defense of his woman.

Sigh. A man coming to her rescue. *Just like one of those romance novels Teena likes to read.*

Luna sidled up alongside her. "What did you do this time?"

Why did everyone assume it was her fault? "I didn't do anything."

Luna snorted. "Sure you didn't. And it also wasn't you who put Kool-Aid in Arik's mom's shampoo bottle and turned her hair pink at the family picnic a few years ago."

"I thought the short spikes she sported after she got it shaved looked awesome."

"Never said the outcome wasn't worth it. Just like I'm totally intrigued about what's happening here. That is Leo laying a smackdown on that Russian diplomat, right? Since I highly doubt they're sparring over who makes the better vodka or who deserved the gold medal in hockey at the last winter Olympics, then that leaves only one other possibility." Luna fixed her with a gaze. "This is your fault."

Meena's shoulders hunched. "Okay, so maybe I'm a teensy tiny bit responsible. Like maybe I made sure my ex-fiancé and current fiancé got to meet."

"Duh. I already knew about that part. What I'm talking about is, how the hell did you get Leo to lose his shit? I mean when he gets his serious on, you couldn't melt an ice cube in his mouth. Leo never loses control because to lose control is to lose one's way, or some such bullshit. He's always spouting these funny little sayings in the hopes of curbing our wild tendencies."

Pookie had the cutest personality. "What can I say?" Meena shrugged. "I guess he got jealous. Totally normal, given we're soul mates."

"Whatever the reason for his snap, he's totally broadcasting a hot vibe. I mean, he's like a brother to me, so I don't really see it, but you should hear the girls at the bar. Between Leo and Dmitri, they're torn on who they think is sexiest."

"They're discussing what?" Meena whirled to glare in the direction of the bar. Sure enough, a gaggle of women clustered, ignoring their dates and other guys in favor of eyeballing the tussling men.

Eyeballing my man.

Grrr.

Time to blow this club.

Before the bouncers could tear the rollicking pair apart, Meena dove into the mess, literally throwing herself between the men. To their credit, they had reflexes honed enough to stop their punches mid thrust.

"Vex, what the hell are you doing? Can't you see I'm busy?" Leo grumbled.

"Do not involve yourself in the matters of men, *lyubov moya.*"

She could now see why people went to jail for murder. The stubbornness of this man was enough to make her violent—intentionally instead of accidentally for once. "Would you stop it, Dmitri? Face it. You've lost. Lost me and this fight. I belong to Pookie now, and as you can see, he's not into sharing." She addressed this to Leo, who looked deliciously rumpled with his messy hair, his skin flushed, and needing a kiss to his slightly swollen lower lip.

"Yeah, Dmitri," Leo taunted. "She's mine. All mine. And the only thing I'm sharing is my shower with her. So fuck off."

A shower? With Leo? Why the hell were they still talking?

"This isn't over," Dmitri warned.

"Bring it, you Russian furball. You know where I live. Anytime you wanna go, come pay me a visit," Leo dared.

"Would you two stop verbally pissing?" Luna snapped as she wedged between onlookers to harangue them. "Some stupid pussy called the cops. Unless you want to spend the night in lockup, you might want to vacate the premises."

Cops? Oh crap, Meena should get out of here. With her

rap sheet, they'd probably arrest her too, just because. Time to leave, but not without Leo.

Grabbing a fistful of his shirt, Meena tugged him in the direction of the door. Given their current minor celebrity status—"Check out the size of the guy who was fighting with that other dude"—she didn't have to argue or shove much to get them through the crowd. The sea of bodies magically parted before them.

Good, because maybe if they moved quickly enough, they could get out of here before the cops arrived and a currently manageable situation turned into a troublesome one.

Look at me, trying to stay out of trouble. Wouldn't her mama be proud? Right after she freaked at Meena for having caused a brawl in the first place. In her defense… Yeah, Meena had none. She'd quite enjoyed the fireworks.

Deny it all he wanted. Leo wanted her.

This time when she laced her fingers in his, he didn't pull away. On the contrary, he clasped her digits in a tight vise. He didn't, however, speak, even once he took over the direction of their flight.

"Where are we going?" Meena asked.

"I'm parked over here."

Over here being a paid lot where a big honking Suburban took up two spots. Aiming his key fob at it, he pressed a button, and the taillights flashed. Meena automatically veered to the passenger side, surprised when Leo came with her.

He opened the door then palmed her waist to lift her in!

Did her astonishment show on her face? "Thank you." It seemed the polite thing to say, even if she didn't actually need any help.

Grunt.

Hmm. She didn't know what that meant so she buckled her seat belt as Leo made his way around the truck and slid into the driver side.

But he didn't start the vehicle right away. He stared out the windshield, fingers loosely gripping the steering wheel.

She waited. *When a man is thinking, you need to leave him alone.* Or so her dad had barked on more than one occasion when her knocking interrupted his thinking time in the bathroom.

When Leo finally did speak, he had a question. "Why is Dmitri so determined?"

"Because he's not a man who likes the word no."

"Obviously, but I meant more, why you? The guy's obviously got some money, he's not bad looking, and he's got power. He could have any woman he wanted. Why is he so obsessed with you?"

It might have miffed another woman to have her man ask what made her so awesome. Given how Leo reacted, he obviously understood her allure, but in this case, Dmitri was less obsessed about her awesomeness and more in love with her… "Hips."

"What?"

"Dmitiri wants me because of my hips. On account of they're wide. As in birthing wide."

Leo blinked at her.

So she explained. "He's a big man so it stands to reason he might make big babies. But he doesn't like the might part. He *wants* big babies. He figures if he, as a larger-sized tiger, mates with a larger-sized lioness, then he's pretty much guaranteed to create a giant tigon. You know, a hybrid of our species, much like you, but in reverse."

"He wants you as a breeding machine?"

She wrinkled her nose. "More or less, which is why I refused to marry him no matter how much money he promises."

"He tried bribing you?"

"Bribing. Threatening. Seducing."

Ooh, that was a definite growl from her man.

She leaned over and placed a hand on his thigh as she stared him in the face. "You are so sexy when you're jealous, Pookie."

"I am not jealous."

"Really? Because I thought that was why you started the fight. Although I am surprised you waited so long after he grabbed my ass to do so."

"He grabbed your ass!"

She quelled his shock with a kiss. Ah yes, there was that sizzling fire she recalled from the last time they'd embraced.

Lips meshed and moved against each other, tasting, nibbling, arousing the senses. She leaned into him as far as she could, her damned seat belt preventing her from crawling into his lap.

Wait, what seat belt? With a click, it wound away, releasing her, and before she could take advantage of the freedom, he'd dragged her over the console.

Given their size, it wasn't the most comfortable fit. The steering wheel dug into her back, her legs dangled over the center console, but who cared? She was in Leo's lap, kissing him, touching him.

And he was touching her.

His hands roamed her body, branding her through the silky fabric of her dress. A big palm slid up her thigh, tunneling under her short skirt.

Fingertips brushed the fabric covering the vee between her thighs. She sucked in a breath. Anticipation tingled along all her nerves.

He rubbed two thick fingers against the wet fabric of her panties. Could he feel that quiver of excitement? Judging by his contented rumble, he had.

Again he stroked, and she mewled into his mouth, a sound he caught and—

Knock. Knock. Knock.

"Hey, Leo, mind giving us a ride once you're done mauling our girl Meena?"

"Go away!" Meena yelled. "I'm busy."

"How long do we need to leave for? Two minutes? Five? I'm kind of hungry and not in the mood to wait too long."

Good thing Leo was strong because the pride might have otherwise lost three lionesses when she dove out the door, ready to kill them.

Then they almost died again when she realized Leo wasn't coming up to her room once they reached the condo complex to finish what they'd started.

Aching, frustrated, and miffed, she did what any self-respecting woman did in this type of situation. She got drunk with her new best friends and inhaled buckets of ice cream.

Then she passed out. Somewhere. Alone.

CHAPTER THIRTEEN

Called to the penthouse suite for a dressing-down. A first for Leo, the rule maker. He was usually the one giving these lectures or the guy who provided the calm voice of reason when Arik ripped into an offender.

Except this time, Leo sat on the couch of shame as the guilty party.

Agitated, Arik paced in front of him, a tall man with an impeccable haircut, courtesy of his hairdresser wife.

"What the hell were you thinking, starting a brawl in public?"

Thinking, not much, at least not with his human head. Primal instinct, however, that was a whole other thing. "Sorry." He did what he always advised others. He apologized.

"Sorry?" Hayder, who'd joined them for this impromptu meeting, laughed. Then laughed some more as he dropped onto the couch beside Leo, who held an ice pack to his aching jaw. Damn that tiger could throw a punch. It wasn't often Leo met someone who could handle him. The bruise was proof of that. As for the ice pack, while the injury would disappear in a day or two, a cold pack would help with the swelling.

Funny how he had not noticed his injuries when making out with Meena in his truck, a make-out session cruelly cut short. Worse, he almost let Meena punish those who dared interrupt them.

He'd also almost roared in his best omega voice for those lionesses to "Get the fuck out of there!" But he hadn't. Only because Meena reacted first.

I deserve this lecture from the boss. He'd lost control and broken the rules, even unwritten ones that he'd made up like "Don't get involved with lionesses," especially ones related to the alpha.

"Sorry. You're sorry?" Arik couldn't hide an incredulous note.

Hayder saved him. Kind of. "Dude, in all the time I've known you, this has got to be the first time I've seen you called in for causing trouble. And over a woman?" Hayder practically rolled off the couch he laughed so hard.

Not just any woman—

"This is over Meena?" Said by Arik in a disbelieving tone several pitches above his last statement. "Meena? Meena, as in my cousin, the walking catastrophe?"

Leo wasn't a cowardly lion to run from the truth. "Yes. The tiger took her from me."

And he'd wanted her back.

"Why didn't you let him keep her? Now, instead, she's caused an international incident."

"It wasn't her fault."

"Was she there?"

"Yeah, but I'm the one who lost my temper." And he'd probably lose it again if that Russian a-hole came near Meena again.

Arik spun on his heel to arrow his gaze at him. "Yeah, you did. And you've caused me a shitload of problems. I mean, you attacked a Russian diplomat on our territory, one with permission to be here."

"He's a criminal."

Arik shrugged. "Perhaps, but that's in Russia. Here he's a business man, one who got attacked by the omega of my pride."

"What do I need to do to fix things?" Apologize? He was a big enough man to do that. Pay him off? He had funds stashed for a rainy day.

"We could give him Meena," Arik mused aloud.

Who growled? Surely not him.

"Oh shit. The rumors are true. She's his bloody mate." Hayder no longer sounded so amused. "No. Say it isn't so. If you claim her, then that means"—he swallowed hard—"she'll stay here. Like forever. Noooooo!"

Hayder wasn't the only one having a melodramatic moment. Arik eyeballed him, a pained expression on his face. "Please, please, *please* tell me you're not actually going to mate with her. I don't know if we could survive having Meena here full time."

"Dude, she's a walking disaster," Hayder commented.

"A magnet for trouble," Arik added while Hayder nodded.

"A hurricane on two legs."

"A destructive force greater than Mother Nature."

Leo held up a hand. "Um, guys, you might want to stop before I crack your skulls together. You aren't telling me anything I don't know, but…" He sighed. "I'm afraid, and I mean really afraid, she might be right. I think she's my mate."

About time you admitted it.

Shove it. And yeah, he didn't care if his liger sulked in his mind. Admitting he might get stuck with the vexing Meena didn't mean he'd give in without a fight.

The moment had arrived for him to flip things around. Time to tilt her off balance. From here on out, he'd take back control, set some new rules, and then have fun making Meena follow them. And if she didn't toe the line he drew, she'd face punishment. A sensual, erotically charged punishment just for her.

Rawr.

CHAPTER FOURTEEN

The bells in hell rang, a cacophony of noise that forced the army of demons in her head to swing their hammers harder.

Oh, make it stop.

Yet the strident shriek kept going. And going.

The ringing stopped.

Sweet bliss. She snuggled her face deeper into her pillow. Just a few more minutes of sleep. Precious slumber… Snore.

A snort cut off as she startled awake at the insistent ringing that resumed. Funny how it appeared to get louder. Closer. Irritatingly close to her face. She batted at the evil electronic device that dared ruin her plan to sleep off her hangover.

Swung and missed. Stupid half-asleep reflexes. She batted at it again. Missed, oddly enough, almost as if the phone had moved, which, given the spins she recalled from last night's copious drinking, was possible. She knew the floor certainly seemed determined to shift under her.

Beep.

It stopped. Thank you for voicemail.

Now she could go back to—

Ring. Ring.

Argh!

Who kept calling? Maybe it was important. Maybe right now she didn't care. All she wanted was for the damned thing to stop its annoying sound. She really wanted to crush it, but her heavy eyelids wouldn't open, which meant the phone lived. For now.

As if annoyed she ignored it, it got closer. *Ring. Ring.* Louder.

"Go away," she mumbled. "Sleeping."

Its annoying chime died once more as it finally went to voicemail.

Then it beeped, again to let her know she got a message. Given she recognized the shrill ringtone, she knew exactly who was sitting on redial.

Sorry, Mom, but I am not in the mood right now.

Having gone to bed late, real late, as she stayed up with the girls drinking and eating, giggling over Leo's abrupt snap at the club, lamenting at how he'd ditched her, she wasn't in the mood to face the day yet. And not even close to wanting to deal with her mother.

Ring. Ring. There it went again. Annoying and loud.

What she couldn't figure out was why her cell phone sounded so damned close. She was certain she'd left it on the entry table when she staggered in last night, having barely managed to navigate the elevator with all its darned buttons.

Floor or table, either way, the phone shouldn't be ringing right above her face in her bedroom. Hey, she'd made it to bed. Bonus!

"Wakey wakey, Vex. Aren't you going to answer? It's

your mother, and this is the fourth time she's called. Would you like me to tell her you're indisposed?"

Hold on a second. It didn't take long for her bleary mind to grasp Leo was here. In her room. About to talk to her mother at—she squinted at her clock—seven in the morning.

Eep.

Her eyes shot open, but before she could flail an arm in his direction and demand the phone, he answered.

"Meena's phone. Can I help you?"

She moaned, her super hearing meaning she heard her mother's very polite, "Excuse me, but who are you, and why are you answering my daughter's phone?"

If this were Meena, she'd say something like "I'm a serial killer, and sorry, but your daughter is all tied up right now. Muahahaha." Of course, the last time she did that, the SWAT team wasn't impressed, and she wasn't allowed to hang out with Mary Sue anymore.

Trust her Pookie to stick to the truth. "I'm Leo."

"Hello, Leo. How are you today?" Her mother ever Miss Manners.

"I am just purrrr-fect. Yourself?"

"Um. Er. Would you mind passing the phone to Meena, please?"

"I would, but she's kind of...*indisposed.*" Did he just smirk at her as he said it?

She frowned.

He grinned. It was a sexy grin, a mischievous grin, but that still didn't prepare her for him saying, "How about I get her to call you back once we've located her clothes? With my help, I'm sure I can get her dressed in no time. Or not." How low and husky he said it, his eyes boring into hers, wicked promise within them.

Of course, that wicked promise would have to wait, given what he'd just said to her mother!

"Are you insane?" she mouthed.

"If I'm insane, then it's totally your fault," he replied, aloud.

Uh-oh.

"Peter! I need you now!" Her mother forgot her manners and yelled for Meena's dad.

Not good. So not good. Poor Leo. And she liked him so much. Even if it was only going to be a verbal barrage, she still yanked the covers over her head so she wouldn't have to witness the carnage as her daddy came on the line. Unfortunately, she could still hear it.

"Who the fuck is this, and what are you doing with my daughter?" Daddy didn't bother with niceties.

"Hello, sir, I'm Leo, the omega for the pride harboring your daughter while her spot of trouble blows over. As to what I'm doing with your daughter, I am trying to keep her out of trouble, but not succeeding very well so far. She has a knack it seems for causing disasters."

Familiar laughter boomed. "That's my baby girl."

At least her father didn't see the havoc that followed her as a problem. Mother wailed she'd never get married if she didn't start to act like a proper lady.

"As to my presence with your daughter, just keeping an eye on her. We've run into a issue with an old beau following her here."

"That Russian prick showed up?"

"Indeed. And events have escalated where I fear there is only one thing to do. It's drastic, but inevitable. " The click of the door cut off the rest of that conversation.

What the hell? She poked her head out, only to note

her bedroom was empty. While Meena hid under the covers, Leo had wandered away.

Still talking to my father.

That couldn't bode well. It never did for her ex-boyfriends. Frederick still crossed the street if they happened to share the same sidewalk.

Scrambling out from under the layers, she bolted to the bedroom door and yanked it open. Popping into the living room, she glanced around for Leo but didn't immediately spot him.

Where had he gone?

The open area didn't leave many places to hide. The door didn't have a peephole, so she swung it open and stuck her head out in the hall.

No Leo.

He wasn't in the half-bath either.

She frowned as she pivoted in the space. Had she imagined him there? Imagined the whole phone call too? Perhaps she was still sleeping.

A sudden gust of air had her turning to see her big man stepping in from the balcony, the drawn drapes having hidden his presence out there.

He no longer held the phone to his ear. Apparently, he was done talking because he had tossed the cell phone onto the couch.

Daddy must not have reamed him too hard because he certainly didn't tremble in fear, or make the sign of the cross in her direction. Still though, she wondered. "What did you tell my father?"

"Morning, Vex. Forget something?"

She almost asked him what until she saw the way his gaze smoldered and caressed her almost naked body.

Oops. Had she jumped out of bed in only her panties?

Nudity wasn't something that Meena usually noted or cared about. Mother, on the other hand, was always yelling at her to put clothes on.

She and Leo had a lot in common. "You should get dressed."

"Why? I'm perfectly comfortable." So comfortable she brought her shoulders back and made sure to give her boobs a little jiggle. He noticed. He stared.

Oh my. Was it getting hot in here?

Funny how the heat in her body, though, didn't stop her nipples from hardening as if struck by a cold breeze. Except, in this case, it was more of an ardent perusal.

Did Leo imagine his mouth latched onto a sensitive peak just like she was?

"While I am sure you are comfortable, if we're to go out, then in order to avoid a possible arrest for indecent exposure, you might want to cover your assets."

"We're going out? Together?"

He nodded.

"Where?"

"It's a surprise."

She clapped her hands and squealed, "Yay," only to frown a second later. Leo was acting awfully strange. "Wait a second, this isn't one of those things where you blindfold me and tell me you've got a great surprise, only to dump me on a twelve-hour train to Kansas, is it? Or a plane to Newfoundland, Canada?"

His lips twitched. "No. I promise we have a destination, and I am going with you."

"And will I be back here tonight?"

"Perhaps. Unless you choose to sleep elsewhere."

Those enigmatic words weren't his last. "Be downstairs and ready in twenty minutes, Vex. I really want you to *come*." Did he purr that last word? Was that even possible?

Could he tease her any harder? Please.

"How should I dress? Fancy, casual, slutty, or prim and proper?" She eyed him in his khaki shorts and collared short-sleeved shirt. Casual with a hint of elegance. He looked ready for a day at a gentleman's golf club.

And she wanted to be his corrupting caddy, who ruined his shot and dragged him in the woods to show him her version of a tee off.

"Your clothes won't matter. You won't wear them for long."

Good thing she was close to a wall. Her knees weakened to the point that she almost buckled to the floor. Leaning against it, she wondered if he purposely teased her. Did her serious Pookie even realize how his words could be taken?

He approached her until he stood right in front of her. Close enough she could have reached out and hugged him.

She didn't, but only because he drew her close. His essence surrounded her. His hands splayed over the flesh of her lower back, branding her. She leaned into him, totally relying on him to hold her up on wobbly legs.

"What about breakfast?" she asked.

"I've got pastries and coffee in my truck. Lots of yummy treats with lickable icing."

Staring at his mouth, she knew of only one treat she wanted to lick.

Alas, she didn't get a chance. With a slap on her ass, he walked off toward the condo door.

Leo. Slapped. My. Ass.

She gaped at his retreating broad back.

"Don't make me wait. I'd hate to start without you." With a wink—yes, a real freaking wink—Leo shut the door behind him.

He was waiting for her. Why the hell was she standing there?

She sprinted for the shower. Only once ensconced in the glassed enclosure did she realize she'd forgotten to ask him what he'd talked about with her dad. The sly liger, he'd diverted her attention. Still though, given Leo had met her with a smile, obviously either Daddy's threats didn't bother him—which was brave yet foolish, Daddy never threatened lightly—or Daddy liked him?

Nah. That would never happen. As Daddy always said, there was no man good enough for his baby girl.

Good thing Meena had a thing about not listening to her parents.

In record time, she'd showered, bundled her damp hair atop her head, and skipped down the stairs, too impatient to wait for the elevator. Unseemly haste, but given Leo could change his mind at any time, she figured it best not to keep him waiting.

Skidding into the lobby, she pretended a decorum she didn't feel. Leo stood along with a few of the pride ladies, the phone held to his ear. He kept his words low, too low for her to hear, not that she would have heard much over the pounding of her heart.

How crazy, here she was nervous about what he had planned. But excitement also thrummed inside her.

She didn't need to speak for him to realize she'd arrived. Turning toward her, he blasted her with a smile.

Holy hell. His smile was more deadly than his fists. She sucked in a breath, poleaxed by the heat that invaded her limbs. No wonder he didn't show his pearly whites often.

The man could start a bloody riot if he used that wicked grin in the wrong place.

Don't touch. Mine.

Her lioness had a very distinct plan should anyone react too familiarly to his awesomeness. Mental note to self: Invest in dark clothes. They hide the bloodstains better.

Leaving the lionesses with a vibrating order of, "Get it done," he strode towards Meena. She could have practically melted at the direct gaze he raked her with.

He stopped a few paces from her. "Ready, Vex?" He held out his hand, and she skipped to him.

"Am I going to like what you have planned?" she asked.

"Very much," he promised.

And that was all he revealed as he led her out the door to his waiting car. But who cared about their destination? He held her hand.

He's holding my hand. It gave her such a giddy, warm feeling inside.

Before anyone snickered, it should be noted that as a larger-sized girl, and tough to boot, Meena had spent most of her life being treated as one of the boys.

In her younger years, she didn't mind. She liked to play rough and tumble with the best of them. Then she hit her teenage years. She shot up several inches and began towering over the guys she knew. She developed breasts, a big pair of them. Things changed.

No longer did the boys treat her as one of the guys, although, mind you, they did still try and cajole her into wrestling, which she quickly came to realize was for a cheap thrill and a grope.

Yes, they noticed she'd become a woman. Yes, they

tried to cop a feel and run the bases. What they didn't do was treat her as if she were delicate. Used to Meena's wild tomboy ways, they didn't hold open doors, or bring her flowers, or do small, intimate things like hold her hand. In their defense, she was taller than many of her boyfriends so handholding was at times awkward.

But she wished they'd try. A teeny tiny part of Meena wanted to be treated as if she were dainty, even if she was like a bull elephant in a china shop—her mother's most oft-heard lament about her youngest daughter.

So, that was why when Leo held her hand, his fingers laced through hers, his thumb stroking her skin, she couldn't help but smile. Leo didn't just treat her with respect. He made her feel like a woman.

He opened the truck door, and as before, he palmed her waist and lifted her in, effortlessly.

As he slid into the driver side, she couldn't help a happy sigh as his essence surrounded her.

"Everything okay, Vex?"

Better than okay. However, given she didn't want to scare him off, or break the spell Leo appeared to be under, she just nodded, biting her tongue for once. Mother would be so proud.

Not much was said as they drove, probably because they spent the first half doing a number on the breakfast he'd brought.

She groaned as she ate the scrumptious cherry-cheese Danish. He growled. She moaned as she sank her teeth into the moist carrot cake muffin with its buttery icing. He grumbled. She couldn't make a sound at all when she offered him the last bite of the custard-filled donut and he sucked the icing sugar from her fingers.

His raspy tongue against her skin totally sent shivers rocketing through her body. And when he sucked the tip?

She almost dove onto him so she could properly maul his delectable body.

But she held off. She showed restraint because her curious kitty truly wanted to see what he had planned.

While they didn't talk much, the atmosphere wasn't strained. Tense a bit, alive with the electrical attraction humming between them, but it was a good tense. Leo put some music on the radio, and when Foreigner came on, she couldn't resist singing, and to her delight, Leo joined her, his deep baritone wrapping her in a sensual velvet glove.

At the end of the song, she laughed. "I can't believe it. You sing."

"No I don't."

"You do too! I heard you."

Again, he shot the most deadly smile her way. "But I will deny it if ever asked. Think of it as my deep dark secret. I like to do karaoke, usually in the shower where no one can hear."

"Why hide when you have a great voice?"

"I also have a membership in the no-pussy club. If I don't want my status as a badass revoked, then singing is out. As is ballroom dancing, buying feminine products, and wearing pastels."

"Sounds chauvinistic."

"Totally, which is what makes it fun."

"Fun how?"

"Because it drives the lionesses nuts."

"I thought you were all about keeping the peace."

A massive shoulder rolled as he shrugged. "Yeah, but that doesn't mean I don't like to have a little fun."

The wink he tossed her had her giggling again. The more she got to know him, the more intrigued she found herself.

They exited the city and drove for a while on the highway, the scenery consisting of pockets of suburbia along with farm fields and wooded areas.

Recognizing a few of the names plastering the exit signs, she suddenly realized where they were going. "You're taking me to the Lion's Pride ranch."

"I am. I thought it might be a good plan to get you out of the city for a bit, let you stretch your legs, and get some fresh air."

A fine plan. They'd no sooner parked than Meena was exiting the truck, not waiting for Leo to come around and hand her out. She took only seconds to strip as a dazed Leo watched.

After the way he'd teased her all morning, she didn't feel bad returning the favor. Her turn to wink. "Catch me if you can, Pookie." With that dare, she changed shapes, calling forth her lioness.

About time, chuffed her feline self as she bounded forward, the pain of the morph a familiar one and quickly forgotten in the elation of her feline form.

She didn't fear any eyes that might watch. Only those the pride approved were allowed on the ranch. It was a safe haven for those who needed an escape from the city and a place to run wild.

Freedom to be themselves within acres upon acres of woods and fields.

On four paws, she bounded to the edge of the lush forest and dashed under heavy branches. The sun-dappled trail beckoned, the rich smells of nature and the muskier scent of small prey an olfactory delight.

Behind her, a roar erupted, not a roar of challenge, more one of, I'm coming to get you.

Yay.

Leo had accepted the challenge. The chase began.

She ran. Fleet paws weaved the forest floor, bounding through the decaying matter littering the ground, brushing branches that hung too low. She favored speed over stealth. Her ultimate intent didn't including evading Leo forever. She wanted him to catch her, pounce her, and take her to the ground because, then, what happened after she really wanted to know.

Something had changed since last night, but she couldn't pinpoint what. Had he come to grips with the fact they were meant to be together? Or was this just another facet to his personality, one he shared with everyone? The genial host entertaining a guest.

Nah. Leo wasn't the type and that meant this, the whole sneaking into her condo, taking her out here was all him. All for her.

I'm special.

And no she wasn't special in a needs-a-helmet kind of way, no matter how many times her brother insisted.

As she ran through the woods, the chirp of birds, the huffing of her breath, and the soft crunch as she hit debris were the only sounds. No more roars, no obvious sign of pursuit, and that was why when a feline body dropped from the tree in front of her, she almost landed flat on her nose as her hind claws dug in, stopping her forward momentum.

Good grief he's huge.

Magnificent, her lioness added.

He truly was. As a lion-tiger mix, Leo possessed attributes from both. His body bore the stripes of a tiger, if much fainter and more golden. His striped tail ended in a dark tuft while his mane rivaled that of any king's, but in a dark shade that highlighted his majestic face and enormous teeth. Teeth he bared.

His freaky version of a feline smile?

Over her initial shock, she feigned nonchalance as she regained her balance and righted herself. With a twitch of her tail, and a toss of her head, she pranced past him.

He swatted her ass.

Oh he did not.

Yes he did.

With this invitation to play, she whipped around and pounced him. But he must have expected it because he threw himself down and let her pin him.

She growled.

He chuffed.

She head-butted him.

He rubbed his nose against hers.

She chomped him then sprang away, leading him on another chase.

Bursting free of the forest, she caught sight of the small lake, or was it a pond? Didn't matter. She remembered swimming in it as a kid. Without thinking twice, she soared at the water and hit it with a splash.

She changed shapes, experience in her swimming pool back home ensuring she held her breath lest she drown in the midst of the morph.

Surfacing, in her human shape again, she drew in a lungful of air before perusing the shore.

The empty shore.

Frowning, she cast her gaze around as she treaded water, seeking a sign of Leo. But it seemed she'd lost him. Odd. Where did—

A hand grabbed her ankle and yanked her down. Mid squeal she went under, clamping her lips tight lest she swallow water. The hand holding her loosened but only so it could take a new position on her waist.

Despite the murky water, she saw Leo, his hair waving with the current they created, his lips quirked in a grin.

With his arm anchored around her waist, he scissored his legs, propelling them to the surface. Their heads broke the skin of the water, and she took in a breath then used it to laugh.

"Pookie, I can't believe you swamp-monstered me."

"I can't believe you screamed like a girl," he teased.

"Maybe I'm more delicate than I look," she sassed.

In the past, those kinds of statements had met with snickering or outright laughter.

With Leo, however, his expression smoldered, and he was utterly serious when he said, "I think you look delectable. And you were positively dainty in that dress last night."

Damn jaw took that moment to unhinge, at least that was the excuse she was using for her prolonged gape. "Dainty? You do know the definition right?"

"Isn't it something along the lines of small and pretty?"

"Yes."

"Then I used the correct term."

Yeah, that earned him a big ol' smooch. A smooch that went on and on as he somehow kept them afloat. Good thing one of them was paying attention because with her legs and arms wrapped around him octopus-style, they would have probably drowned if they counted on her to keep their heads above water.

Thankfully they didn't drown, and Leo proved the smarter one as he'd maneuvered them during their discussion to shallower water, or at least shallow enough that he could plant his two feet and truly enjoy the kiss.

The kiss wasn't the only enjoyable thing. Despite the cool temperature of the water, their skin made contact and rubbed. And rubbed. Oh how she loved the sensual slide of their flesh together. The temperature of the water might have proven chilly, but they didn't feel the cold. Their inner fever, born of arousal, kept them warm.

Whilst her legs clamped him tight, her sex could only pulse against his lower belly. Meena wasn't a shy girl, or innocent. Need made her quiver, especially since she felt the evidence of his desire popping just under her butt.

She squirmed, trying to adjust her position, but he kept her too tightly clamped. "Not yet, Vex."

"But I'm *hungry*." She pursed her lips in a pout.

He kissed it away as he waded through the water, the level dropping as it got shallower.

Air and sunlight caressed her bared skin, but what she really wanted was for him to caress her. And he did, of a sort.

His big hands cupped her buttocks, keeping her aloft, her body wrapped around him like a second skin.

Their lips nipped and tugged as they embraced, the hot pant of their breaths the only discernible sound.

The heat of her passion burned hot, hot enough that she, once again, tried to pry their bodies apart far enough to give him an invitation. He still wouldn't let her move, but he did release her mouth long enough to whisper, "Are you ready, Vex, for my big surprise?"

"Am I ever."

"I've been waiting all day to give it to you," he murmured against her ear lobe.

"Then give it to me. Give it to me now." She'd burst if he didn't take care of her.

He chuckled, the rumble vibrating against her skin. "I know you're hungry."

"So very, very hungry," she agreed.

"And I'm hungry too."

"Then what are you waiting for? I'm ready." More than ready. Dying for him to stop this yearning. Craving his touch. The bliss.

"Awesome. I can't wait to show you what I brought for our lunch."

Lunch?

Lunch!

CHAPTER FIFTEEN

Her bafflement would have made him laugh if he wasn't as tortured as her.

Close. So close they'd come to succumbing. It wouldn't have taken much, just a nudge and a push. She'd shown herself more than willing. But...

He'd made a promise to her parents to not physically claim her unless they were mated. And no, it wasn't her father's threatened, "I'll tear your intestines from your body, use them to bind you, then skin the fur off you to make a coat for my wife," that made him respect his word. Leo had also made a silent promise to himself that he would treat Meena with a respect he sensed she didn't often enjoy. Under Meena's wild and wicked manner lurked a woman, one who longed for the same courtesy and flirtation that she saw others receive.

He would give that to her.

Giving is good. Give her anything she wants. His liger's vision of giving was of a more carnal nature, and hard to ignore, especially with Meena still plastered to him. So much delicious flesh.

Wanna taste.

Can't. Even if it hurt—and it hurt a lot—he was a man of his word.

Setting her on a blanket spread under a tree ahead of time, atop a soft bed of mossy grass and undergrowth, he ignored her mewl of disappointment.

It didn't help he almost caterwauled too.

Turning his back on her for a moment, he searched for the towels he'd also asked to have stashed when he called in his picnic order to the ranch the night before.

He found towels all right, hand towels. Someone's idea of a joke.

Not so funny, given that meant he had nothing to cover Meena with. Nothing to hide her curves.

Don't look. Don't look.

As if he had that kind of willpower where she was concerned. He turned.

Wanna see.

What he saw was her glaring at him. Such a rare expression on her usually happy mien.

"You did not just stop the most awesome makeout session ever for lunch."

Awesome? Okay, so his chest might have puffed out a little. "Not just any lunch. A great one. I had the kitchen pack us some fried chicken made last night. And everyone knows fried chicken tastes better the day after."

"You have a point about the chicken. However, I've got throbbing girly parts that are screaming for some action."

Her outspoken honesty, while initially jarring, now quite pleased him. Meena didn't hide the truth. She said what she felt, and what she felt was desire for him. Mental fist pump. And, no, he wouldn't pounce and lick her for the compliment.

He tried to rein things back. "Such impatience, Vex. You do realize the most titillating part of anything is the buildup to the main event?"

"You've already built me enough, dammit, Pookie. A girl can only take so much."

"Would it console you to know my man parts are also throbbing"—most painfully and visibly—"and yet, while I could indulge in a quick taking of your"—gulp—"beautiful body..." There went his train of thought for a moment. Her fault as she leaned back on her elbows and hit him with a come-hither stare. She also pushed her shoulders back and presented her breasts. Sob. He needed to focus. Maybe if he explained she'd understand why the hell he wasn't jumping on her—now. "Surely you see the merit in taking things slowly. In savoring our budding attraction—"

"Budding?" She snorted. "Try more like exploding. Or at least I would have if someone had given me a few more minutes."

"Think of it as extended foreplay."

"Screw foreplay. I want sex."

That made two of them. Exactly why the hell had he made that promise? "Speaking of orgasm, look what else I brought to go with the chicken." As he kneeled down on the spread blanket, he flipped back the lid to the basket—courtesy of the folk who maintained the ranch. After laughing, then asking if it was a joke, then laughing again, they quickly cooperated with his picnic plan when he threatened to show them how human pretzels were made.

Despite herself, Meena craned forward, her boobs swaying enticingly. Curse him for having morals and making promises.

"Are those chocolate orgasms?" she asked.

It shouldn't make a grown man shudder to hear a woman say the word orgasm. Yeah, it didn't stop a tremor from rocking him, especially since no longer submerged by water the musk of her arousal scented the air. "Good girls can have all the orgasms they want." He growled it.

"Good girl?" She uttered an extremely wicked chuckle. "Oh, Pookie, but I'm best when I'm bad."

With those words, she leaned back and changed position. Not to hide her assets or make things easier on him. Of course not. She knew exactly what she did judging by her naughty smile as she sat cross-legged on the blanket, still utterly naked.

Why was he resisting? He should go over there and ravish her like she demanded. Weren't her wishes more important than any silly promises?

Stop concentrating on her naked parts. Focus on something else. Like lunch. Yeah. If they were eating, then he couldn't lust, right?

He handed her a linen napkin, and she laid it across her lap, hiding one part of her but leaving her glorious breasts exposed. Knowing what hid under the tiny scrap of fabric made him want to go diving for cream.

Bad kitty.

He ripped the lid off the container with the chicken and offered it to her. She grabbed a hunk and tore into it.

Leo prided himself on his iron control. He wished someone would have warned him that one woman could turn it into a puddle with just one groaned, "Damn that's good chicken."

Determination to respect her turned out to be torture for him. Every bite. Every moan. Every peek of her pink tongue as she licked her lips.

He flung himself on his back with a groan.

Immediately, she straddled him, which really didn't help matters. In all his planning, he should have brought clothes. Or maybe some armor. What possessed him to think he could handle a morning and afternoon alone with her? Why had he promised not to rush things?

"Pookie." She sang his name as she nipped his jaw. "Oh, Pookie. You can't hide from me. Why are you fighting this so hard?" To prove the hard point, she rubbed her slick cleft against his erect shaft.

"Vex, no, we can't. I promised."

"Who did you promise? My dad? Oh please. He doesn't get to decide who I have sex with."

"I promised myself, too, to treat you like a lady."

"You have been, but even ladies like a bit of passion. A bit of…" She nibbled her way down the column of his neck and nipped at one of his flat nipples. He sucked in a breath. "Fun."

"I gave my word." And much as pleasure beckoned, he wouldn't betray it.

"And what did you say exactly?"

"That I wouldn't have sex with you unless we were properly mated."

"So mate me, then do me."

"Vex!" His eyes shot up to shoot her a shocked look.

"What?" She failed the innocent look, but then again, who wouldn't, given she'd slid even farther down his body and now knelt between his knees, one hand gripping his cock.

"You shouldn't—you can't—Oh fuck." What else was there to say when the woman you wanted most wrapped her lips around the head of your shaft and sucked?

Oh how she sucked and tugged at his erect cock. Her

lips slid the length of his steel pole, caressing him, encasing him in liquid heat. He couldn't help but dig his fingers into the blanket, fighting to hold his hips still lest he begin to thrust in the sweet cavern of her mouth.

But Meena wasn't interested in his impressive control. As with every other moment since they'd met, she seemed determined to smash his resistance. To bring him places no one else brought him, both emotionally and physically.

She deep throated him.

Deep. Throated. Him.

No one had ever done that before, not with his somewhat impressive size. Meena did, though, and she did so with gusto and the most gorgeous mien. Her lashes fluttered darkly against the tops of her cheeks, and her eyes closed as she enjoyed herself. Her lips were opened wide around his dick, their perfect pinkness a distinct contrast. Her cheeks hollowed as she suctioned. And oh, the sounds she made. Sweet sounds of pleasure. Soft growls of enjoyment.

Could he stop a bellow as she took him to the brink of ecstasy and then shoved him over it?

Yeah. Forget a man with iron control. He shot his creamy load into her welcoming mouth, and she took it. She took every ounce of him and didn't stop sucking until, in a hoarse voice, he pleaded, "No more. Damn it, Vex, you're going to kill me."

Thing was he couldn't die yet. No way. He had a favor to return.

What about the promise to not claim her?

He would keep that promise. His dick wouldn't sink into the velvety heat of her sex, but by hell, his tongue would!

"Get on your back." Did his tone contain an element of command? Damned straight it did. This was one time he needed her to listen.

"Oh goody, I get a turn too."

How delighted she sounded. Her refreshing attitude and lack of coyness was utterly enchanting. She didn't hide her sensuality or desire. She embraced it and spread her thighs that he might take a turn kneeling between them.

Utter perfection. From her tousled hair framing her face in damp wisps, to her heaving breasts topped with fat berries, to the indent of her waist and wide flare of her hips. She was his ideal woman.

She is my woman.

Mine.

And even if he wouldn't brand her with his cock or mark her with his teeth, by hell, she would feel the lash of his tongue.

But only after he had a taste of the breasts he'd dreamed of.

Leaning forward, he dipped his head to tug at an erect peak. Her back arched, and she let out a moan.

"Yes. Oh yes. Suck me."

He'd known she'd be vocal, and he loved it. Loved that she didn't fear telling him what she liked.

Around her nipple, his tongue circled, wetting the skin, feeling the ridges of the puckered peak. He sucked the tip into his mouth. Nibbled her. Even nipped her.

She liked that, or so he assumed given she yanked on his hair and practically smothered him when she held his face so tightly to her breast.

Good thing he was stronger. In this, he would have

some control. He switched nipples, lavishing the same attention on the other as she panted and mewled encouragement and demands of "More. Don't stop. Oh gawd. Yes."

As delightful as her breasts proved, though, the true treat was farther below. Letting his lips leave the splendor of her bosom, he trailed hot kisses over the swell of her belly and still farther down to the very short thatch of blonde covering her mound.

He couldn't help but nuzzle her. A hot sigh left her.

"Oh, yes. Please. I mean no. You shouldn't." Her hands pushed at him. "I don't want to hurt you."

Hurt him? It hurt him not to taste. Kneeling between her legs, he paused a moment and looked at her. She did appear quite worried if the wrinkle between her brows was any indication. And yet, he could see the honeyed desire on the lips to her sex. "You want this."

"Yes, but I can't let you. I might forget myself in the moment and cause some damage. It's happened before."

"You can't stop me." With those words, he fitted his hands under her ass cheeks, loving the plump handful. He raised her from the blanket, angling her for his pleasure—and hers. Then he gave her a long, wet lick the length of her sex, from the peeking hood of her clitoris to the entire seam of her cleft.

Her musky cream hit his taste buds and exploded, as did she. Her hips bucked, and it was only by sheer strength that he kept her anchored.

"Sorry," she squeaked.

"Don't you ever." Lick. "Apologize." Suck. "For your passion, Vex." Nibble.

With each caress, she gasped, moaned, or cried out.

Her body shook. Her legs draped over his shoulders, and her heels dug into his back.

He feasted on her, letting her wild passion take him on a journey he'd never imagined. Never a selfish lover, Leo always took care of his partners, but with Meena, he didn't just want to pleasure her. It pleased him so much too.

Despite the recent ejaculation, his shaft swelled, throbbed, and begged him to sink into the pink heat and thrust hard. Deep. Fast.

Claim her. Mark her. Take her.

Oh fuck. Oh yes. He couldn't have said if he thought it, or she chanted it. Either way, he swayed in time to the thrusts of her hips as he lapped at her. He hummed against her sex, "Come for me, Vex. Come against my tongue."

And she did. She screamed loudly, long, and lustily as she let her climax take over. Her thighs squeezed his head in a tight vise. He could see why she feared hurting him, but he could handle it. She was his.

To prove he didn't mind her strong passion, he kept on sucking and nibbling, wanting more. Because he needed more, more of her. He wanted to imprint her with his touch. To quench this insane thirst he had for her.

A second orgasm rolled through her before the first was even done. Her second scream was more of a hoarse croak, a testament to the mindless pleasure holding her in its throes.

How he wanted to join her. And he meant join with her. His body buried to the hilt within her welcoming sheath, breaking all his promises. Indulging in selfish desire.

Argh. In one swift movement, he dropped her still

quivering body onto the blanket, gently of course, and Leo ran to the water. He dove in and let the cold liquid caress his steaming parts.

But the chill water couldn't solve his problem.

Only Meena could. And only if they were mates.

CHAPTER SIXTEEN

I can't believe he didn't claim me.

He'd come so close. She was sure of it. Meena blamed her father. It was his fault Leo wouldn't take that final step. Making Leo promise not to debauch her. What the hell?

Was everyone determined to pussy block her?

At least the raging inferno was down to a dull throb. Her man had come through and given her the tongue lashing of a lifetime. Even better, he didn't require a CAT scan to check for brain swelling. Nothing like a trip to the emergency room for a mood killer.

Anyhow, after Leo's swim, no amount of smiles, boob jiggles, or innuendo would get him to budge. But the good news? He was aroused, which meant he noticed. Noticed and did nothing about it!

She didn't know if she liked him because he was so determined to respect her or wanted to stake him to the ground and ravage him. Okay, maybe a bit of both.

Despite the taut sexual energy between them, the afternoon passed pleasantly. It turned out they had many things in common, particularly a love of sports, both watching and playing, although their NFL teams were division rivals. It would make for interesting Sundays in the fall.

And yes, she planned to be around when the seasons changed. Just like she intended to be with him for Christmas and make him buy a potted tree because, while she didn't like artificial pines, she also couldn't stand the thought of chopping a live one down for decoration. So, every year, she bought a live pine tree, and once Christmas was done, she kept it watered and healthy until spring when she could plant it.

As they lay on the blanket, her head pillowed on his stomach, his fingers lazily threading her hair, he finally asked her. "How did you and your sister get such a reputation? I swear Hayder practically has convulsions when your name is mentioned."

She shrugged as she stared up at the cloudless blue sky. "My sister and I don't go out trying to create disasters. Things kind of happen around us."

"Happen?" He snorted. "Care to rephrase that? From some of the stories I heard, the pair of you are quite the pranksters."

She laughed. "I guess. But no worse than our male cousins. They just didn't get caught as often. It doesn't help that some of our antics backfired. For example, Kenny and Roger put Uncle Gary's car on his roof, and it's boys will be boys. Teena and I do it, and we're grounded for a year and working for our uncle every weekend and all summer. And all because our uncle didn't get his parking brake fixed. Like we were supposed to know it wouldn't hold the car. We never expected the car to slide down, tear out the chimney, hit the back deck, and flip into the pool, which caused a mini tsunami and flooded their basement."

Leo's body shook, a faint tremor she couldn't help but feel since she lay on him.

"You getting cold?" she asked.

"No," he said in a choked voice. "It's just…" He burst out laughing. "You really aren't lucky. I've done the car thing. Usually it's no more harmless than paying for a few roof shingles."

"You, involved in a prank?" She couldn't stop a melodramatic grab of her heart.

"Aric and Hayder liked to involve me in their shenanigans, whether I agreed or not. They were a little rambunctious during our college days."

"Only a little?"

"Okay, a lot, but they've calmed down."

"Must be boring for you," she remarked.

"Boring? No. It's a relief not to constantly have to keep an eye on them and clean up their messes. It leaves more time to relax and read a good book."

She made a gagging noise. "Even you sounded bored telling me that. No wonder fate had us meet. You need me, Pookie. Need me to keep you on your toes and give you purpose."

"A man would have to be nuts to want chaos on a daily basis."

Turning her head, she grinned at him. "Congratulations on joining the ranks of insanity."

He shook his head lightly, given it was pillowed on his arm. "You have the utmost faith we'll end up together. I have to ask, why? Aren't you worried that you're in for some celestial joke, given how some of your other ideas turned out?"

A rare moment of sadness turned her lips down. He raised a valid point. It did worry her that her trust and belief that Leo was the one would turn out to be false. What if he couldn't handle her? What if he ditched her or ran screaming one day? It had happened before, so many times she'd lost count.

But Meena wasn't a person to live forever what-if-ing. She had faith and refused to give up. "I am worried. I know my history with men. I remember the name-calling and their terror and the restraining orders. Yet, despite all my bad luck, I believe there is a happily ever after out there for me. That you will be that happily ever after. My gut and heart say that you will be the man who can handle me and all my catastrophes." To herself, she silently added, *And perhaps, one day, despite my flaws, you'll realize you love me.*

Such a serious speech, too serious for her to remain still, especially with Leo regarding her so intently, the pity clear in his blue gaze.

She didn't want his pity.

I want his love.

To her feet she sprang. It was her turn to sprint for the water, less for a cool off than to hide the tears that trembled.

People all thought her so damned strong. They assumed she didn't care about the jokes and mishaps. They joined in with her false laughter when yet another boyfriend dumped her.

Some things stung even the happiest of people.

No unhappy thoughts. Snap out of it. Her kitty tail whipped her mind. Her feline didn't suffer from any doubts that she was awesome. Live for today, live for the moment, never let fear win.

A motto she lived by.

The coolness of the water helped distract her thoughts. A darting shape made them wander further.

Fish? Almost as tempting to a feline as a warm puddle of sunlight.

Off she darted, feet fluttering and arms pulling, chasing after a shadow in order to escape her qualms.

A large shadow paralleled her. A twist of her head and she saw Leo had come to join her.

Out snapped his hands, cupping them in a closed ball.

Had he caught it?

Kicking in the direction of daylight, she popped her head from the water, and he rose as well. He didn't say anything about her admission. He didn't offer pity—not even in the form of a kiss!

What he gave her was even better. The normalcy of friendship. "I caught it."

"No you didn't." Of course she argued—with a smile.

"Did too. You're just jealous."

Was Leo teasing her? "Damned straight I am, Pookie. Jealous of every woman who eyes your fine body."

"You're trying to distract me. It won't work. I have the fish." He raised his cupped hands from the water. Liquid streamed. "I think I should win something."

"Like?" Treading water, she reached out to pull his cupped hands down a bit more. She held them trapped between their bodies. She hovered close, her legs moving in the eggbeater pattern she'd learned as a child when taught how to swim. Doing it in close proximity, enough that she could lean in and brush her lips over his, though, took some maneuvering. But she managed it.

Lips sliding over his, she whispered, "Tell me what you want, Pookie, because I know what I need. I'd like to feel your hands stroking my body. Those rough fingertips, the sign of a man unafraid to work and get dirty, tracing my skin. I want your body pressing against mine, naked, pinning me, making me vulnerable to you. I need"—she sucked at his lower lip—"for you to sink your cock into me. To stroke me, deep and hard. I want it *hard*. From a real man, one who can handle me. And fuck me. And give me what I crave." She stopped, staring him in the eyes, loving the intentness of his gaze. "I. Want. You." She tilted her head and struck, teeth nipping the strong column of his neck that hovered above the water.

How low the groan sounded, a deep rumble from within him.

Did he even notice his actions as his arms split and came around her?

She noticed. Popping her cupped hands from the water, just before his squeeze, she crowed, "Aha! Now who's the better fisherman?"

The rich laughter poured over her in a husky, molasses vibration. She shivered, and she lost a bit of focus as that sensual languor returned. Her hands parted, and with a *plop*—and probably the fishy version of a fuck you—the little fish returned to its home, darting away as fast as it could wiggle.

"Looks like we're tied," he said, not at all angry she'd tricked him. Dear God, was that a dimple in his cheek, a small one, but combined with the twinkle in his blue eyes, her heart almost stopped.

"Does that make us both winners?" she asked. They could exchange a prize. A sixty-nine went two ways.

"Tiebreaker. Betcha I can make a bigger splash than you with a cannonball."

She snorted. "Pookie, you are delusional if you think those tight glutes of yours can spray more water than this ass of mine."

And so they spent the rest of the afternoon playing. Best damned time she'd had in years. Even better, her accidents didn't bother Leo one bit. When she tossed a pile of mud at him, hitting him in the chest, he didn't freak out because the slime she tossed had a leech in it. Nor did he scream as if a brain-eating zombie was after him when she wrestled the bloodsucking critter off his skin.

Although she did feel a little sheepish when he reminded her they had salt in the picnic basket.

Leo could also handle her rambunctious side. A good thing, or she might have really hurt him.

When she saw his bare back as she climbed the rocks for a dive, she jumped on it, only realizing as she soared through the air that she might cause some serious damage.

He barely stumbled as she hit him, and she kissed him when he said rather dryly, "Next time can you at least yell Geronimo?"

Next time?

Hell yeah.

Unfortunately, they couldn't remain by the pond forever. As afternoon waned, her tummy began to rumble. The picnic basket was bare.

"Feed me," she growled as she pawed through the empty containers.

Instead of telling her to think of her waistline and getting punched in the face, Leo said, "Me too. Wanna head back? They should be setting up the barbecues soon for dinner."

Singed meat? He didn't need to say anymore.

Swapping skin for fur, she led the way back to the main house for the ranch.

Emerging from the woods, she noted cars parked all over the place. While not shy about her nudity, even she wasn't so brazen as to shift with that many strangers around. Especially considering, if she shifted, Leo might too, and she didn't want him showing off that gorgeous bod of his.

Mine.

Almost.

Darned man obviously wanted her, and yet he held back. Why? Why! WHY!

Frustration, of the mostly sexual kind, refused to stay quiet. Her mental state, however, was quite pleased at how things were progressing. She and Leo were getting to know one another as people. Dare she even say friends?

During the picnic she'd learned so many things about him, tidbits he'd shared, which, in turn, encouraged her to share what it was like growing up as the less-than-dainty daughter of a true Southern belle.

She'd even broached the subject of her twin sister, who while identical in appearance, was nothing like her in attitude. Teena might be known as trouble but only because her softer nature often screwed her over.

Free the kitties at the shelter because Teena couldn't stand it that they might get euthanized, and the cat population went haywire to the point that the city had to call in help to capture and spay them.

Get her dress caught in a cab door, have the vehicle pull away, rip the clothes from her, leaving her clad only in panties and bra. Not Teena's fault she caused a four-car pileup.

Teena was still embarrassed by that incident, and yet Meena was totally envious. She'd only ever caused a three-car pileup on her best day.

She followed Leo's furry behind around to the back of the rambling ranch, or was that mansion? Hard to tell given the original structure had birthed so many additions over the years it resembled an odd hodgepodge of homes stuck together.

Decades past, the pride had lived within its walls. However, as the modern world took over, and jobs in the country grew sparse, as did social events, many chose to move to the city, taking over the condominium complex downtown to eke out lives in a concrete jungle.

But the pride still kept this symbol of their past, and it was where the clan gathered whenever big functions were planned, and by the looks of things, something big was about to happen.

Slipping into a robe, one of many kept on hooks by the rear entrance—again, one of many in this jigsawed home—she noted the hustle and bustle as people arrived with luggage and boxes. Many also held high plastic-draped hangars, suits and dresses for some fancy shindig.

Turning to Leo, who had just finished belting the massive terry cloth cover-up, she asked, "What's going on?"

"Family wedding tomorrow."

"How come I didn't hear about it?"

He shrugged. "It was kind of last minute."

"Am I invited?" And yes, despite his claim it was a family wedding, she felt as though she should ask, given her current ban from some functions within certain branches of the family.

His lips twitched. "As far as I know, you're expected to go. So try and behave between now and tomorrow."

"Maybe you should stick close to keep me out of trouble."

"I doubt anyone's capable of doing that."

"Good point. But I still think you should stick close."

"And why is that?"

"Because if I've got to wear a dress, then I'm not wearing any panties."

How she loved his soft rumbled, "Vex!"

Tucking her into his side, he navigated them through the people milling around, for the most part ignoring their nods and hellos. An omega on a mission. He led them to a set of stairs that took them past the second floor and onto a third. The hall, with its oriental-patterned runner, provided a quiet respite from the uproar below.

"Where are we going?" she asked.

"Lucky for you, I scored us a suite."

Us? As in both of them? The door on the end proved their destination, and he flung it open to display a cozy sitting area and one kick-ass bed.

One. Bed.

Fist pump. "Pookie, you are da bomb!"

"Am I going to fear the answer if I ask why?"

She rolled her eyes. "For having the forethought to get us the room with like the sturdiest looking bed ever."

"Who says we're both sleeping in it?"

"Me, of course."

"Only if you're good. So do your best while I pop out for a bit. You should find some clothes and stuff in the bathroom."

"Where are you going?"

"To locate my own clothing and make sure they've got

enough food for me. Someone helped me work up quite the appetite. It shouldn't take too long. I'll be back in thirty minutes or so."

With a wink in her direction, he left.

She smiled and hugged herself. What a wonderful day so far.

After all the attention Leo had shown her, and the way he was acting now, she had a feeling her gut was right. He was the one.

But he'd left.

So what? He promised to come back. She hoped he did. Nothing sucked worse than waiting on an empty stomach for a date that never showed.

Car troubles indeed. The blatant lie from the date that stood her up totally justified her use of sugar in his gas tank.

No need to plan anything evil for Leo. Leo would come back.

He's my mate.

Or would be soon. She didn't think she could handle this whole respect thing much longer. Either he'd have to bend his morals to ease her desire, or he'd have to claim her and still ease her desires. One way or another, forget about waiting.

The massive bed drew her eyes. Made of thick, sturdy pine logs, it screamed rustic, tough enough to handle just about anything. It also relayed another message if he chose this room. *I think he might be done waiting as well.*

Was tonight the night?

Did he intend to mate her?

Minutes ticked by as she stood staring stupidly in space, daydreaming of her liger. More specifically on that mattress covered in soft blue bamboo sheets.

Leo will be coming back soon.

Time to get her ass moving.

Popping into the bathroom, she noted a hanger on the hook behind the door, its contents shrouded in a zippered plastic bag. First, though, a shower. Shampoo and soap beckoned, as did the razor she pulled from a fresh pack. The hot water sluiced the remnants of the pond from her skin, leaving her fresh and clean.

Good enough for a certain liger to eat.

Towel drying, she peeked around to see what she had to work with. Much like a hotel, the bathroom boasted a hair dryer and some basic hair products, meaning she managed to somewhat create a presentable do. A very high ponytail that would swing like a whip if she danced. Given she could hear the distant thump of music as someone DJ'd some tunes, dinner would be followed by dancing.

I wonder if I can get Pookie to dance with me again.

She emerged from the bathroom with the garment bag in hand and placed it on the bed. Yanking down the zipper, she giggled to see a familiar dress. Someone had packed the same short dress she'd worn when she and Leo had made out in the change room of the clothing shop. How providential that it was the one brought for her to wear tonight. Even odder, it came with a bra but no panties. She dumped out the bag and shook it. She even returned to the bathroom to look but returned empty-handed.

Leo's influence?

Surely not her Pookie. However, she couldn't help a spurt of heat at the thought he might have had a hand in making sure she was bare bottomed under the loose skirt.

Locating her purse on the dresser, she returned to the

bathroom and shut the door because the last thing she needed while applying eye liner was to be startled. She managed a quick tune-up to her face. A light eye liner to darken her eyes, mascara—applied twice because the first time she clumped them shut—lip-gloss, cherry flavored because that was Leo's favorite fruit.

As she smoothed the dress over her body, skimming her hands over her hips, she couldn't help but take a deep breath.

It has been just over thirty minutes. She'd eyeballed the clock on the nightstand before coming into the bathroom. She'd spent at least five minutes in here but hadn't heard anyone enter the room during that time. Leo wasn't there. Disappointment crept up on her, waiting to pounce. Her lioness snarled it back into submission.

She should wait a little longer before allowing herself to believe he hadn't come. Perhaps he'd gotten delayed, or…

Pussy.

Cowardice wasn't her thing. And she was hungry. Either Leo kept his word or didn't. Hiding in the bathroom would change nothing. Out she charged, only to hit a brick wall.

She reeled back, not only because she'd smacked into Leo's chest. She mentally reeled.

He came back.

That more than anything shook her off balance, and she went over—*someone yell timber*.

She didn't fall alone.

Her flailing hand caught Leo's shirt, her foot somehow tangled around his ankle—totally accidental, really—and together they hit the floor. Although, somehow, she ended on top of him. The man had rolled his body at the last moment so he took the brunt of the fall.

What have I done? How badly had she squashed him? *Please don't let him cry.*

She hated it when they cried.

"You okay, Vex?"

He lived! She raised her head and beamed his way. "You're not screaming."

He arched a brow. "Why would I be?"

"We hit the floor kind of hard."

"Hard is right," he grumbled. "But not in the way you think."

Surely he didn't imply... She squirmed into a better position to check—*we have confirmation of an impressive erection.*

He sucked in a breath.

Dammit, had he lied about her injuring him? "Are you hurt, Pookie?"

"I am hurting bad, Vex. Want to kiss it better?" His wink had her lips twitching.

"I am beginning to think I misjudged you."

"Misjudged me how?" Rolling her to the side, Leo got to his feet and then hauled her up.

"You are much more wicked than I gave you credit for." She grinned. "That is so freaking awesome."

"Not as awesome as you in that dress, Vex." His appreciative sweep of her appearance brought a heat to her skin that made her want to trip him and land atop him again. She doubted she'd ever tire of his appreciation of her plentiful curves.

His speculative gaze, though, was nothing compared to her greedy perusal of him. Yummy.

Dressed in form-fitting jeans and a deep purple shirt that brought out the dark highlights in his hair, he looked good enough to eat, and she was suddenly famished—for him.

She pounced. He remained standing, having caught her enthusiastic bounce. He was also more than ready and willing for the hot smooch she planted on him.

Lip-gloss be damned. She smeared it all over his mouth as she tasted the wonderful virility that was all Leo.

She could have kissed him all night. Screw the barbecue and festivities. She had everything she needed right here. With him.

Alas, he apparently didn't want to miss the party because he pulled back.

"We should get moving. We're expected."

"Being late is fashionable."

"Being late also means we only get dinner scraps."

"Good point. We should hustle." She didn't protest when he placed her back on the floor.

"Aren't you forgetting something?" He stared at her bare toes.

"What about my toes?"

"Aren't they missing something?"

"Did you change your mind about having me dig them into your back as you give me oral?"

One tic under the eye? Check. She was getting to him.

"I meant they're missing those." He stared pointedly at some heels by the door.

She sighed. Loudly. "You mean I have to wear shoes too?"

"This is a semi-formal function."

"You are way too serious, Pookie.

"I resent being called too serious. I'm just as carefree as the next guy."

She snorted as she slipped on her heels. "Prove it."

"I didn't wear a tie."

"Bah. I'm not wearing any underwear," she announced as she sashayed past him into the hall.

It wasn't the smack on her ass that had her stumbling but rather his claim of, "Neither am I."

CHAPTER SEVENTEEN

As Meena skipped down the stairs, Leo thumped after her. Her panty announcement wasn't unexpected. After all, he'd told Luna quite specifically not to pack any when she brought her some clothes. But now, watching Meena bounce, so much of her legs exposed, he wished he'd made her wear them. That skirt was awfully short.

Too short.

Too accessible.

And the bed was getting farther away.

Exactly why had they left the room?

Oh yeah, food. If they had any hope of surviving the night, they should eat. He didn't want her lacking for energy later.

Not that he planned any debauchery.

Why not?

Because tonight wasn't about them sneaking off and stealing kisses among other things. This evening's celebration was a precursor to a couple's new life. A party with friends and family before the seriousness on the morrow.

A wedding. Blech.

Like any proper-minded male, Leo dreaded weddings like every other man. But in this instance, he'd make an exception, for Meena. He knew she'd enjoy the ceremony. He just wondered what kind of catastrophe to expect.

Exiting onto the main level, he could have laughed at the reaction Vex wrought. It seemed his date for the night was well known.

"Meena!" Squealed in a happy high pitch.

"Meena!" uttered with reedy panic by someone who bolted.

Since her admission that afternoon, Leo felt even more attuned to her than before. He noted the slight stiffening of her back as the callous asshat hurt her feelings.

It seemed cousin Marco had yet to forgive her for hitting him in the face with a hockey puck a year or so before she'd gotten banned. And yes, Leo knew the story. Everyone did. Marco could hold a grudge, but how well could he take a punch? They'd soon find out because Leo planned to teach his cousin forgiveness later.

First, he snared Meena's hand and strutted with her to the lineup of long tables covered with platters of food.

They'd arrived early enough to get some choice pickings. Times two. The folks handling the barbecue made sure to pile his plate with a few burgers, the patties thick and juicy.

Leo found a seat, a pair of chairs actually, but having a spare one available didn't stop him from yanking Meena onto his lap, the ominous groan of the chair be damned.

It seemed he wasn't the only one to hear the threat of the unhappy seat. "Pookie, we're going to end up on the ground. We're too big to both sit in this chair. I'll just sit in the one beside it."

"Fuck the chair. You're staying on my lap."

"But why?"

"Because I like it." He loved it when he managed to surprise her. The shape of her mouth so evocative.

Before she could ask another stupid question, he stuffed a roasted potato bite in her mouth. She nipped his finger in the process then smiled.

"Yummy. Again."

He gave her a crisp cherry tomato. The purse of her lips before she sucked it in mesmerized.

There was no more question after that of not sharing the seat. They fed each other, and if the occasional passerby who chuckled or snickered happened to trip over his size-fifteen feet, not his fault. A man needed to sometimes stretch his long legs.

The buzzing voices of the pride, and those who'd traveled in at a moment's notice, rose in a hum around them. Leo didn't pay it much mind. He was more intent on the woman in his lap, who watched the action around her with parted lips. He could see and sense her happiness as people wandered over to say hello. Even Great Aunt Cecily, "Who must have finally forgiven me for pulling all the wires out of her bras so they wouldn't poke me when she grabbed me in a bear hug."

Alas, they couldn't remain on their own for the entire evening. As third man on the totem when it came to pride matters, it was no surprise at one point to see Hayder beckoning Leo.

"I gotta go see what he wants," he said, setting Meena on her feet. "I'll try and not be long. How about I snag us some drinks on my way back?"

He left her with a kiss on the lips and a slap of the ass. Hey, the damned thing was made for smacking.

He wasn't gone long. Really, not long, but it proved enough time for Meena to find trouble.

Or, in this case, cause it.

Time to pull an omega.

CHAPTER EIGHTEEN

Time to take things to the next level.

Leo is the one.

It wasn't only Meena's inner feline that insisted. The woman believed it too. Not only had Leo not ditched her when given the chance, he'd insisted she sit on his lap where he hand-fed her some tidbits. Finger-licking good.

A pity about the crowd. The hard erection poking at her bottom, distinct even through his pants, could have used a good lick.

Later. A later that couldn't come quickly enough to suit her. This afternoon's teasing, far from appeasing her lust for Leo, had simply made it stronger. Poor Leo would have to bend his morals and promises a little because she wasn't taking no for an answer.

Tonight's the night, Pookie.

As soon as they got through this party and Leo returned from whatever task Hayder summoned him for, she would drag him off and have her wicked way with him.

Rawr.

A cat whistle left her pursed lips as she watched Leo saunter away. Damn did that sweet ass of his in those form-fitting jeans make a fine sight.

I think I'm in love.

Or someone drugged the food because this giddy lassitude and urge to grin like a maniac about to go on a murder spree proved unstoppable.

She'd never been happier, especially since, when Leo left, he didn't do so with unseemly haste or eagerness. On the contrary, he seemed miffed. How dare the world interrupt them?

Now the biggest dilemma was how to pass the time while she waited for his return. *And I need to be good.* He wanted her to behave. Surely she could manage that for a few minutes?

Seeing a gaggle of women, including Zena and Reba, she wandered over. "Hey, bitches, what's happening?"

"I don't believe it. Surgeons managed to separate them," Zena exclaimed. "I was beginning to wonder if someone had doused the pair of you in crazy glue."

"You mean like the time I did that to Callum?" Her first boyfriend at thirteen didn't appreciate her crush. So what if it took a few hours of their conjoined hands dipped in acetone to separate them? A smart boy would have totally used that time to get to first base instead of freaking out.

"To this day he flinches if someone tries to grab his hand," Reba remarked. "So what's up with you and Leo? Are you guys like a couple now?"

Given his public display? "Totally."

"Leo, though, really? Of all the guys I thought you'd hook up with, I never expected him."

Meena stuck her tongue out. "Go ahead and be jealous. I don't blame you. My man is awesome."

"Or he's been taken over by body snatchers. Seriously, Meena, we ain't never seen him act like this. How the heck did you get him to fall for you like that?"

Oddly enough, by being herself.

Meena chatted with her cousins, doing her best not to gush overly much about Leo, but as she talked, she noted a pair of women, one of them almost as tall as her, but slimmer, with perfectly coiffed hair and painted face. She and her friend kept peeking at Meena then snickering until she finally asked, "What's so funny?"

"Nothing." Bursts of laughter.

Meena glanced down at herself but saw nothing amiss. "Did I drop food on myself again?"

"No."

"Then what?"

"As if you couldn't guess." Big blonde shrugged. "It's just…you and Leo."

"Yeah, what about us?"

"I mean, you and Leo, seriously?"

"Yeah, what about it?"

"It's just, you're so different. He's so Leo, you know, prim and proper. While you're a walking disaster on two legs. Honestly, I don't know what any man would see in you."

The stranger raised a valid point. Yeah, they were polar opposites, but she thought that rather complemented them. However, having this woman point it out and feeding on Meena's insecurity of before didn't sit well.

Instead of taking her frustration out on the bitch for pointing out her weakness and accidentally rapping her face off her knuckles, Meena thought it best to leave. She'd act mature for once. She'd behave and make Leo proud.

At least she meant to. But then…

"That's it, walk away, fat ass." Derisive snort. "And this is supposed to be the big and bad Meena I've heard about? Ha. More like the ugly cousin no one wanted around. Poor Leo. Maybe I should show him he doesn't have to settle for scraps."

Did that bitch just threaten to make a move on my man?

Red rage! Red rage! And there went all her plans to behave.

Before the bitch could blink, Meena was on her. Literally.

She took the other blonde down in a tackle that wrung an, "oomph," from her. Grabbing a fistful of hair, she rapped the girl's head off the ground.

"Don't." Smack. "You." Evade tearing fingers. "Lay. A. Hand." Head, meet the ground again. "On. My. Man." Oops, there went a hunk of hair.

While Meena initially had the advantage of surprise, the other blonde, no delicate thing herself, quickly recovered and spat back. "You fucking bitch! I am going to scalp you."

And thus did they end up rolling on the ground, trampling the grass, tearing at each other's hair, not managing any really powerful punches because of their close proximity to each other.

It didn't take long for Meena to recover the upper hand. In this case, she straddled the mouthy girl's upper body. She'd just pulled back her fist to deliver a sweet blow when a strident whistle sounded, and a voice stopped her dead.

"Vex, what the hell are you doing?"

CHAPTER NINETEEN

The catcalls and screams didn't surprise Leo, nor did discovering Meena at the heart of chaos. There was his delicate flower, on the ground wrestling Loni, a lioness who'd come to town for the wedding. The same Loni who'd made numerous passes at him over the years, but whose high maintenance attitude made him steer clear.

He wondered what had triggered the hair pulling and wrestling. He also really wished, once again, that Meena had worn panties. The occasional flash of her girly bits dragged the possessive side of him out—which really wanted to snarl, "Mine. Don't look." It also woke the hungry lover that wanted to toss her over a shoulder and take her somewhere private for ravishing.

At least those closest to the fight and witness to her bare bottom were all women. The bad? They were all women. His usual method of smacking a few heads together to save time wouldn't work in this situation. Boys shouldn't hit girls.

So how to stop the catfight?

He stuck fingers in his mouth and blew, the whistle strident and cutting through the noise. In the sudden quiet, he said, "Vex, what the hell are you doing?"

Meena, fist held back, poised for a serious blow, froze. She swiveled her head and smiled sweetly. No sign of repentance at being caught misbehaving. "Just give me a second, Pookie. I am almost done here."

He arched a brow. "Vex." He used his warning tone. "Maybe you should let Loni go and forget about hitting her."

"Probably. But the thing is, I really want to smash her face in."

Sensing an out, Loni turned her head and whined, "Get this crazy bitch off me. I didn't do a damned thing. She started it. She always starts shit. She should have never been unbanned. She's trouble. Always has been."

Reba and Zena opened their mouths, ready to leap to Meena's defense, but Leo raised a hand. They held their tongues—not an easy feat for cats—but their eyes spoke quite eloquently.

Leo focused his attention on Meena. "Vex, is this true? Did you jump her?"

Her shoulders slumped. "Yeah."

"Why?"

"Does it matter?" she asked.

"It does to me. Why do you want to rearrange her nose?"

"She said we didn't belong together and that maybe she should show you why she's a better choice." Meena couldn't help but growl as she recounted the reason for her ire aloud.

"Punch her."

To say a few mouths O'd in surprise would be an understatement. No one was more surprised than Meena at his order. "Seriously?"

"Yeah, seriously. Given any idiot with eyes could see we were together, then that makes what she said mean and uncalled for. If you're going to talk the talk, then you have to be prepared to pay the price. Since I can't very well smack Loni for causing trouble, as pride omega"—and, yes, he thrust out his chest and put on his most serious mien—"I am giving you permission to do so."

Permission granted, and yet Meena didn't hit Loni. On the contrary, she stood, smoothed down her skirt, and tossed her head, sending her ponytail flying.

"No need to rearrange her face. You just admitted in front of an audience we are together. That calls for a round of shots. Whee!" Meena did a fist pump and yelled, "In your face, bitch!"

Sigh. Wondering at his mental state that couldn't help but desiring the most erratic woman he'd ever met, Leo downed the beer in his hand then snagged one from Luna who passed to his left. He drank hers too.

The evening was young, and he'd need help if he was to survive—without dragging Meena off somewhere for some serious debauchery.

How delightful she appeared tossing back some shots, dancing to the various tunes belted out by speakers placed around the football-field-sized yard. Given the trouble she could cause—if she flirted too long with any one male—Leo remained close by but didn't dance. He wasn't sure he could control himself if he got too close to her. He didn't need to deal with the snickers and comments if he chose to cart her off into the woods to have his wicked way. Actually, he was more afraid she might drag him off and have her wicked way.

I need to keep my word. But forget about keeping his sanity. He'd lost his mind the moment he met her. Lost a lot of things, but oddly enough, he didn't lament their passing. Change wasn't always a bad thing.

His liger roused with a warning growl. *Watch yourself.*

Despite all his warning instincts urging him to turn and face the approaching threat, he didn't budge when a very large man came to stand beside him.

"You Leo?"

"Yup."

"You're the one my daughter's got her mind set on?"

"Yup."

The other man grunted. For a moment, they both stared in silence. "Just so you know, that's my baby girl."

"I know."

"She's fucking delicate," Meena's father rumbled as his daughter stomped her foot on the ground to a song, got her heel stuck, yanked, broke the heel, teetered, and fell, knocking a tray of drinks from a passing waiter's hands.

"I will keep her from harm." Even if that harm was sometimes from herself.

"If you ever make her cry, I will hunt you down and skin you myself. I can fetch a fine price for liger's fur on the black market."

The threat didn't even make him blink. "While I cannot condone the murder and sale of a pride member, I can appreciate your sentiment, sir. But no fears. It is not my intention to make her cry." Scream, yes, but that would be in pleasure and wasn't something he felt a need to divulge.

"You've been warned." With those final words, the

man melted back into the crowd and left Leo to his vigil. For a while longer, he watched Meena, amused at how disaster loved to lurk around her. But despite her mishaps, nothing could ruin the smile on her lips.

Except for the arrival of one guest.

CHAPTER TWENTY

Hips swinging, arms swaying, Meena partied. It had been quite some time since she'd enjoyed a full-on family celebration, especially one she was allowed to attend.

The entire backyard area was packed with people making her wonder where the hell they all planned to stay. She knew that, other than the original farmhouse, the property boasted a few cabins for those who liked a spot of privacy, and she spotted a few tents in the distance, but she had to wonder how many would end up on couches, floors, and, heck, passed out on the grass.

Felines weren't always picky about the spots they chose to nap. Even a tree would do in a pinch.

She didn't have to worry about where she was sleeping tonight. A certain liger made sure of that. Speaking of Leo, where the hell had he gotten to?

For a while, she'd sensed and seen him watching her, witness to her suave dance moves. She just wished he'd have joined her.

Then again, this type of family function probably wasn't the right place for the dirty dancing she had in mind.

As the dusk gave way to night, she decided to find her big man. So shoot her for being a girl, but she wanted the reassurance of his smile and perhaps a sweet kiss. Yes, she also planned to grope his fine body, a reminder to the ladies present that he was spoken for.

She waved and grinned as she passed familiar faces, some of whom shouted, "Meena!" and raised their glass in toast. A few made the sign of the cross, and one woman whispered, "Are you sure our insurance will cover us?"

Accidentally land on the hood of a car, crushing it because of a fluke bounce off a trampoline, and Aunt Flore never forgot it.

Given the amount of folk milling about, she wondered who the hell this pre-celebration was for. Leo had mentioned some kind of impromptu wedding on the morrow, but she'd yet to figure out who the bride and groom were.

Perhaps it was Arik finally making his little mate, Kira, his legal wife. Apparently they were living in sin for the moment, or so her mother tsked. Apparently shacking up was on the list of things a lady shouldn't do. It totally made Meena want to do it just to hear that special tone her mother reserved for her.

Alas, no man was crazy enough to attempt not only the danger of living with her but no one dared cross her dad. Daddy's favorite shirt said, Go ahead and mess with my daughter. I ain't afraid to go back to prison.

Perusing the crowd, she spotted the pride's beta, arm looped around his wolf mate. She doubted this wedding was for the recently joined Hayder and Arabella, who apparently had skipped off to Vegas one night and returned hitched a la Elvis style.

So who were the happy couple?

Meena doubted she'd ever do the whole wedding thing. For one, despite the fact that she knew Leo was her mate, he didn't seem the type to want the chaos of a white wedding. Not to mention, she and white just did not get along. If she was going to drop some salsa, then it was landing on her boob, each and every time.

Besides, she could just imagine the destruction she would wreak if she ever wore the same type of big flouncy gown her mother wore at her own wedding. She would probably take out a few dozen guests if she turned the wrong way.

On second thought, that sounded like fun. Mental note to self: get a huge wedding dress for Halloween and go to a party as a dead bride.

Pleasantly mired in her own thoughts, she didn't note the lunging hand until too late. Someone gripped her arm and spun her around. Reflex made her punch the offender, only to hit a rock-solid wall. Just not the wall she'd hoped to see.

"Oh, it's you."

"Your joy in my appearance overwhelms, my love." Dmitri relinquished his grip on her arm to clasp at his chest.

"You want to see joy, turn around and walk away."

"Leave? But I've just gotten here."

"Why are you here? Is this another sad ploy to try and kidnap me again?"

"You say that like it's a bad thing, and yet, aren't many

women's romances comprised of abduction and seduction?" Dmitri waggled his brows in a failed attempt at sexiness.

"You're not a Viking, and I'm not a fainting damsel. So no. And, besides, I'm taken."

"So I hear, and yet"—he took a sniff—"I still don't scent a mating mark."

"Leo's not a rushing kind of guy. He likes to take things slow. Build up to the main event. You know, foreplay and whatnot." Tease and denial, enough to drive a woman mental. Or at least more mental than usual.

Dmitri shot her a grin. "I can give you foreplay, and pleasure. Much more than that big lug ever could."

She rolled her eyes. "Oh my gawd. You just don't give up, do you?"

"Not when the prize is you."

"You mean my birthing hips and excellent genes?"

"One and the same."

"I am not going to help you start a dynasty of giant babies."

"I never said you had to be willing."

"And you wonder why you have a hard time getting a woman." She rolled her eyes.

"You know, it is precisely that attitude that has made me revise my plan to abscond with you and make you my bride."

"About time. But if you're not here to kidnap me, what the heck are you doing here then? And why isn't anyone tossing you out on your striped ear?"

"I was invited."

"Who was stupid enough to do that?" she asked.

"I was."

Spinning on her heel, she finally found Leo, holding two bottles of sweating beer, one brown and skunky, the other pale with a wedge of lime shoved inside the glass. She grabbed the dark one and chugged it before he could saddle her with the girly one.

Once she'd satisfied her thirst—without belching because she was, after all, a lady—she asked, "Why did you invite the king of misogyny?"

"So I could show him this."

This comprised of Leo spinning Meena in his arms and plastering her mouth with his. A surprise smooch. A welcome lashing of tongues. An unimpressed audience.

A gagging noise ruined the mood. "Is that necessary? I've already withdrawn my suit for the lady."

"Just making sure you get the point," Leo remarked when he came up for air.

"And to think I'd heard you were the sporting one," Dmitri said in a dry tone of voice.

Leo fixed Dmitri with a stare, a cold and menacing one. So hot. "I might be sporting, but I play to win. I also don't share. Meena is mine."

She was? Screw the zoologists that said lions couldn't purr. Her inner feline was definitely making a happy noise.

She flung her arms around Leo, not just because she was so happy right now but also because that last beer, on top of all the shots, was making her kind of woozy.

"Is it me, or is this field tilting?"

"I think someone is ready for bed." Scooping her into his arms, Leo proceeded to carry her away from the party.

To those who shouted ribald remarks—as if she needed any ideas when it came to debauching her serious liger—

Leo fixed them with a stare. Apparently he was one omega who didn't need to rely on his voice to have people obey.

They made it to their bedroom without mishap, her strong man actually carrying her the entire way in an impressive display of strength. A good thing, too, because Meena was finding it hard to keep her eyes open.

Fatigue and alcohol seemed determined to conspire against her. Like hell. This was her night. The moment she'd waited for. She wasn't about to let something like a spinning room and eyelids dragged down by cement blocks get in her way.

As Leo leaned down to deposit her on the bed, she tightened her grip on him, not letting him pull away.

"Kiss me," she demanded.

"I shouldn't."

"Shouldn't didn't stop you earlier this evening."

"Earlier this evening you weren't incapacitated."

"We can work it off. If we take it slow, I'll be fine. Just don't expect me to swing from a chandelier. The last time I did that, the whole ceiling came down," she confided.

"I'd really rather not hear about your sexual exploits," he growled.

A jealous Leo was adorable. "Oh, I didn't do it for sex. We were playing Tomb Raider. And I would have gotten away with the treasure, too, if the bolts would have held."

"You are something else," he muttered, brushing the hair from her face, his strokes so gentle.

"I'm yours," she muttered as her lashes fluttered shut, her battle with them lost.

"Indeed you are, which is why I'm so sorry I have to go."

"Go?" Her eyes popped open, barely. Sleep yanked on

her, begging her to succumb. "You're not leaving, are you?"

Serious blue eyes met hers—four of them. Damn those Jell-O shots! "I have to if I'm going to keep my promise. I don't trust myself to stay with you. You are much too tempting. Which is why I drugged that beer."

CHAPTER TWENTY-ONE

Admitting what he'd done brought a wince to Leo's face but a look of astonishment to hers.

"You drugged me?" She blinked. A long, slow blink. The drug tried to take her over the edge.

He tried to explain. "I had to. It was the only way I could keep my promise."

"But this was our room. You said so," she slurred, lashes fluttering against her cheeks.

"It is." Make that would be. Tomorrow, everything would change.

"You are so…so…"

He hushed her with a kiss, a kiss full of longing, pent desire, and an affection he would have never imagined for this woman a few days ago.

Meena. A walking, talking whirlwind, who made him feel so alive.

How could he explain how much not touching her hurt him? How could he let her know that he regretted his promise, that he wished more than anything he could peel that damned dress from her body, run his hands over her silky body, and claim her with every ounce of his being. Stamp her with his mark.

I want to make you mine.

But he couldn't. Not yet. Would she understand? Would she forgive him? "Just one more night, Vex. Trust me."

Snore.

She'd lost her battle with the sleeping agent he'd slipped into the beer.

He leaned his forehead against hers, closing his eyes for the moment. *I hope she forgives me.* His actions seemed extreme, even to him.

Why couldn't he just claim her and give them what they both needed? Who the hell drugged the woman they wanted to claim instead of breaking a stupid promise?

He did.

Damn me. The things he did because of respect—and love.

I need a fucking beer. Make that a keg. However, he doubted there was enough booze to drown the caterwauling of his inner feline.

Stuff it, or I'll let Clara weave ribbons in your mane the next time we shift.

Pink ones.

CHAPTER TWENTY-TWO

Meena awoke to someone sitting on her chest. Given it crushed and impeded her ability to not only breathe but sleep, she finally understood why it irritated her brother when she did it. Especially when the sitter chose to whip the pillow out from under head and smack her with it.

Prying open an eyelid, she glared at Zena. "Why do you want to die?" Forget waking in a happy mood. She only too clearly recalled last night with Leo drugging her so he wouldn't have to have sex with her. Stupid, respectable jerk. Someone was taking his promise a little too far.

Especially since all he has to do is claim me and problem solved.

But he chose instead to walk away.

Doesn't he want to claim me?

She'd certainly thought so but now had to wonder given his actions.

Her inner lioness gave her a mental smack. *Of course he wants you. Who wouldn't?*

What the hell was up with the self-doubt?

I'm awesome.

So awesome he'd left, and now she was being tortured by demons, also known as her favorite cousins.

Zena flicked the tip of her nose and grinned. "Well, good morning to you too, drama queen. I see somebody's in a bad mood."

"You would be, too, if you got drugged and put to bed."

Zena snickered. "I still can't believe Leo did that. Most guys would have just locked you in a room and told you to behave."

"As if there's a lock that could hold me."

"That's what I told him," Reba announced as she flounced onto the bed. "That's why we tossed some sleeping pills in that last beer you drank."

"You aided and abetted him in pussy blocking me? I thought we were friends," Meena accused in her most aggrieved tone.

"We are, which is why we totally approved of his plan. It's nice to see a man determined to respect you. We thought you'd appreciate it."

Sure, make him out to be the hero. The good guy. Meanwhile, that didn't help her aching libido.

"So you drugged the beer."

"Just the one."

Meena frowned. "What do you mean just the one? How did you know I'd drink it? He offered me the pale ale. I took his instead."

A wet raspberry sprayed Meena. Wiping at her face, Meena glared at Zena who laughed, completely unabashed. "I knew you'd do that. Like hello, pale ale is for pussies."

"I can't believe you chugged it though." Reba shook her head. "The stuff hit you faster than we expected. Leo barely made it up here with you before you were snoring."

"But he didn't stay." Stupid gentleman not taking advantage of her.

"Nope, because he said he didn't trust himself to," Reba relayed with a sigh. "It was so cute. You would have loved how frustrated he looked."

A frustration she wanted to cure, except one honorable omega kept fighting her.

"I love how concerned he was about making sure you were safe. He bribed me and Reba to guard your comatose ass while he proceeded to drink and play cards with your father and that Russian fella."

"My dad is here?" A rare frown creased her forehead. How come she'd not known her father was coming for a visit? Wasn't he still supposed to be on vacation?

"Yup, he's here and your mom too. I heard your sister should be arriving sometime this morning as well for the wedding."

Ah yes, the stupid wedding. As if she wanted to envy the happiness of another couple when her own man would rather dope her than shag her. "Ugh, do I have to go? I'd rather mope in bed."

"Are you insane? You can't stay in bed. You'll miss all the fun. Get your ass moving. We've got to get ready."

"It's just past the butt crack of dawn. How long do you think it will take to throw on a dress and some lip-gloss?"

"You've got a heck of a lot more than that to do. You need to shave your pits and those hairy things you call legs."

Damn shifter genes. Men complained about five o'clock shadows. She got the bristles only hours after shaving her legs. Epilation was the only thing that lasted more than twenty-four hours.

"She also needs to eat."

"Good point. She should probably do that before the shower so that she's fresh for when the hairdresser gets here."

"Hairdresser? What do I need one of those for?"

"To do your hair, silly. And then there's the makeup artist."

She didn't argue too much about the artist since she and eyeliner did not get along. "Why do I have to wear makeup?" she whined. "Why are you torturing me?"

"Well, you want to look pretty for your wedding day, don't you, silly?"

Meena blinked. A few times actually. Usually, she would have had a clever repartee, but she was currently speechless—a rare occurrence that deserved a mark on the calendar. She processed Zena's words. They didn't make any sense. Unless…

"I am not marrying that stubborn tiger. Did Leo or my dad lose me to him in a game of cards or something?"

"No. Your marriage isn't because of a lost wager," Reba snickered.

"No matter. I don't care what Dmitri's threatened Arik with or how much money he's offered to bribe the pride. I will not marry him."

"Dmitri? You mean the hot Russian dude? He would have been my first choice, but alas for you, you're stuck marrying big, old, boring Leo today."

"Leo? I'm marrying Leo?" Surely she imagined the words. She must still be asleep. This was obviously a dream. Meena slapped herself.

Reba screeched, "Dude, what are you doing? Your

bruises from last night's catfight with Loni are barely healed."

"I thought you said I was marrying Leo today. I was just making sure I was awake. I'm coherent now, so you can stop screwing with me and tell me who's actually getting hitched."

Zena grabbed her cheeks and stared her in the face. "You. Are. Marrying. Leo. Today. In like hours. So stop fucking around."

Last night, he'd drugged her so he wouldn't have to claim her. Today, he planned to marry her? "But how? Why?"

"Apparently, when your dad made Leo promise to not like deflower you—"

A snicker from Zena. "Too late for that."

"—Leo said if a mating was what it took, then by hell, you'd get mated. But said more nicely of course. Then apparently your mom got involved, stole the phone as a matter of fact from your dad, and told Leo to not waste time and do it now before he changed his mind, that you were lucky to find a man. Then your daddy said, you were, and I quote, 'fucking perfect and if Leo truly cared for you then he'd treat you like the fucking princess that you are.'"

"Daddy said that?" Of course he did. Daddy's affection for his girls didn't see the clumsy feet. "Wait a second, how do you know all this?"

"Well, it wasn't on account of us eavesdropping," Reba said with an innocent stare at the ceiling.

"This is Meena we're talking to, idiot. We totally spied on Leo when he was talking to your dad down in the lobby before your picnic. It's how we got roped into making the plans for the wedding. A wedding you're going to be late for if you don't get your fat ass out of this bed and moving. Shower now while I call down to see where the hell your breakfast is."

She was getting married.

I am getting married.

Holy shit.

She dove under the covers.

"Meena, what the hell are you doing?"

"I can't get married."

"Why the fuck not? I thought you said he was your mate."

"He is."

"Well then, what's the freaking problem?"

Meena poked her head out long enough to announce. "Do I really need to spell it out? Me. A long dress. A walk down an aisle in front of people. A priest. Can you imagine the disasters that might entail?" Tripping over her own gown. A passing bird pooping on her head. Fumbling her vows and saying something really wrong in front of a priest. Getting hit by lightning. Fainting in shock and killing the groom. The possibilities were endless. "I can't do it. Someone go tell Leo that I'll be his mate, but I won't subject anyone to the torture of a wedding."

"Meena, Meena, Meena. You're not thinking clearly. Of course you want a wedding. For one thing, it is what every girl dreams of."

True.

"Second, this is a great way to show all the women in the pride he's your man."

Yeah, hands off, bitches.

"Third, he went to a lot of trouble getting this done in like twenty-four hours. Our sweet and calm Leo was barking orders last night apparently to make sure everything was fucking perfect for his dainty woman."

"He called me dainty?"

"He might have been drunk by that time. But yeah, he did."

"And lastly, you have to do this because I've got a hundred bucks riding on this."

"You were betting I'd get married?" How like her friend to have her back and want the best for her.

"A hundred bucks says you make it down the aisle, but when you toss the bouquet, you start a cat fight."

"At my own wedding?" Meena smiled. "Count on it."

"Especially since that bouquet is mine," Zena announced.

"Like hell. I call dibs."

And thus did her wedding morning devolve into a practice run for the predicted battle later.

But for once, Meena didn't join in. She had a wedding to get ready for. A man to impress. And body parts to shave because, after the wedding, she was clubbing her liger over the head and dragging him to this bed.

No more excuses. Once they said I do, she would do—him.

Rawr.

CHAPTER TWENTY-THREE

I'm getting married.

    Thunk.

Fuck me.

Thud. His head hit the wall again.

No fuck her.

Hmm, that sounded a lot better. He refrained from giving himself a concussion until he remembered…

I'm getting mated.

Bang.

Oh hell this is going to happen.

The tiny thread tethering his mental control snapped.

Panic. Run.

He anchored his feet with the help of his liger—who really thought he was acting like a big, old domesticated pussy about the whole mating thing.

Breathe in. Breathe out. He took a moment to sort his emotions, a cluster of turmoil unlike anything he'd ever encountered.

It was one thing to plan the event—make a few phone calls and set the cousins to work getting it all ready while he kept Meena occupied. But the realization now hit him that this would happen. His life was about to change. Forever.

Eep.

Thankfully no one bore witness to his unmanly squeak. But he heard it, and he didn't like it, which meant he needed to do something about it.

Prying apart the panic and fear currently wringing his whole body took some work. Yet once he managed to shove them aside, it surprised him to discover those emotions that screamed for him to run didn't have a firm root. His trepidations were like smoke and mirrors, a mask to hide...nothing in truth. While he did have a man's healthy terror for matrimony, underneath it all lurked an excitement about what would happen.

After today, Meena will belong to me. Even more intriguing, I'll belong to her. Did possessive pride make any sense? It did now.

Mine. All mine.

Today and forever.

How could he have thought that was scary? Fear could go jump off a cliff—just not in front of Meena because she'd probably follow.

She truly was an awesome kind of crazy. A crazy he couldn't wait to taste. Another thing to look forward to was the evaporation of the barrier holding him back from Meena. Once mated, nothing could stop him from tossing his new bride over his shoulder and carting her off to that sturdy bed. Hot damn, in only a few hours he would finally give her the claiming she deserved.

If she forgave him for what he'd done.

Drugging her might have proven a tad extreme. In his defense, he'd snapped. Rationality, cool composure, control, all the things that made him who he was, that made him an omega, didn't work where she was concerned.

Much like a dry piece of timber, he ignited in the face of her burning presence.

Except to lose himself in her, to claim her like this in the throes of lust, would rob Meena of a chance before friends and family to see him publicly promise himself to her. To show her she hadn't just chosen him. He had also chosen her.

Leo couldn't allow that, so he cheated. He pissed off the woman he expected to marry, hoping against hope that Hayder was right when he said it was easier to beg forgiveness than ask permission.

For a moment Leo wondered, would Meena punch him like he slugged Hayder the last time he'd tried that line of crap on him?

If she did hit him, then he deserved it. He'd take any punishment so long as she forgave him his extreme act and married him today.

Approaching the stairs to the third floor, he peeked up, debating on whether he should go talk to her now before the wedding or pray Meena came walking down the impromptu aisle.

Then he remembered the superstition about not seeing a bride on her wedding day. Did he dare tempt Lady Luck today of all days?

Better not. He'd have to hope the Meena he knew would laugh at his actions and skip down the aisle to throw herself at him.

Was it silly to admit he enjoyed her trust that he would catch her each time?

Turning around, he almost uttered an unmanly yell as

he noted someone had managed to arrive behind him without notice. Clamping his lips, he confronted a tray with steaming food held by none other than his bride-to-be.

It took him aback, which was why he blurted out, "What are you doing fetching your own breakfast? Aren't Reba and Zena giving you a hand? They promised they'd help you get ready." Leo eyed Meena, wearing a floral-printed summer frock, and frowned. "Didn't you like the dress the pride ladies chose for the wedding? They assured me you would. That it was your style." While he'd let the women choose the actual gown, he'd insisted—mostly because Meena's mother seemed adamant—that his bride wear white. A rushed wedding didn't mean Meena had to skimp on tradition, something his future mother-in-law went on to explain in detail before Peter, Meena's father, got on the line and barked, "Do it right. Or die." Which seemed to be Peter's answer to many things, especially where Meena was concerned. "If they screwed up, I'll make them fix it, Vex."

Eyes wide, she gaped at him. "I think we need to clarify something. I'm not—"

He interrupted her before she could finish her I'm-not-marrying-you. "Hold on a second. Before you say anything, hear me out, please. First off, I'm sorry I drugged you last night."

"You drugged me!" How surprised she seemed. Had the stuff that knocked her out wiped a few of her memories?

"Don't get mad. Or get mad, but at least understand I drugged you only because I knew I couldn't keep my hands off you. It was the only way I could think of to keep my promise. To give you what you deserve."

"Are you telling me you want this? That you want to get married?" She arched a brow, and he couldn't hold her gaze. For the first time in his life, Leo found himself truly nervous. Here was a situation he couldn't hit, wrestle, or order into compliance.

Baring feelings was all well and good, but talking about them sucked. But there came a time in a man's life where he had to suck it up and gush, especially when he was a blind idiot for a while. "Would I be going through all this trouble if I didn't want to get married? Listen, Vex, I know we got off to a rocky start. In my defense, you're a little much for any man to handle. Not that I mind," he hastened to add when her second brow shot up. "I like who you are, and I'm a big enough man to admit I might have reacted poorly when you declared I was your mate and that I couldn't escape."

"I said what?" Again, she gaped in open surprise. Then laughed. Pretty damned hard as a matter of fact.

He frowned. "Don't you dare deny it, Vex. You had me all but in front a preacher within five minutes of us meeting. And it scared me. But you were right about us belonging together, even if it took me longer to realize it. You are the one for me, Meena. The chaos to balance my serenity. The colored rainbow to enrich the grayness of my current life. I want you, Vex. Catastrophes and all. I just hope, even after what I've done, and the fact I might sometimes have a stick up my ass, at least according to Luna, that you'll forgive me and still want me too." He ended his gush of words and stared at Meena hopefully, and a little fearfully, given she once again stared at him slack-jawed.

Would she say something?

She did, just not from her lips. No, Meena's voice came from behind him.

"Oh, Pookie, that has got to be the most beautiful thing I ever heard."

Either Meena had some mad ventriloquist skills or… Leo froze as he stared at the woman in front of him, a woman that he realized the more he stared was Meena and yet not. This one wore her hair in soft curls around her shoulders, a tiny scar marred the tip of her chin, and her scent…was all wrong. However, the body that jumped on his back and the lips that noisily kissed the flesh of his neck? That was his Vex.

What the hell? "Who are you?" he asked.

The Meena clone grinned and waved. "Teena, of course."

"My twin," Meena added against his ear.

"Identical twin?"

"Well, duh. And it's a good thing too, or I'd be a little miffed right now that you just said all those beautiful things to her."

"I thought it was you."

"Apparently. It happens a lot, which I totally don't get. She looks nothing like me."

"I feel like such an idiot." He tried to crane his head to see the Meena clinging to his back, but she slapped her hands over his eyes. "No, you can't look. It's bad luck."

"But…"

"No buts. Although I will say yours looks awfully delicious in those pants. But it will look even better when it's naked and wearing my teeth marks."

"Vex!"

"I know. I know. Don't start something we can't finish. Consider yourself warned, however. As soon as that priest says I do, your ass is mine. All mine." Such a low, husky promise. "Come on, Teena, you are just in time to help me get into my gown. Can you believe my Pookie arranged all this?"

The pride in her voice made him smile, but he did have to shake his head at the whole twin sister thing. With one last kiss on his neck, Meena whispered, "See you in a little bit, Pookie."

A little bit was actually about two hours. Two hours of last-minute preparations, the use of his omega voice to calm down some hung-over pride women who wouldn't get along—*Ladies who don't behave get dish duty*—two hours of anticipation, back slapping, and ribald jests.

It seemed like an eternity of hell, but finally, the moment arrived. The field outside had transformed. At the far end sat a makeshift altar presided over by a priest, not of any human church but an official when it came to shifter marital matters—and sanctioned by the state according to his certificate printed off the Internet.

The pride had truly come together in a short period of time. Chairs were layered in rows, well over a hundred of them, set in two columns framing a path upon which someone had unrolled a veritable red carpet.

An arch, woven of branches and threaded with flowers, presided behind the altar. The same flowers overflowed from garden pots placed every few rows for color. Most everyone had arrived and seated themselves. Dressed in their finest, they'd come together, even if some of them still held a grudge because, in their world, a wedding between shifters was always a cause for celebration.

As for Leo, he awaited his bride. Dressed in a tux, with tails of course, Leo stood at the top end of the aisle with his best men, Arik and Hayder. As if he could choose between them.

Tiny Tommy, a cub of almost four, fidgeted in his spot,

the ring pillow bouncing precariously. The rings, however, didn't budge, safely pinned to their spots.

The hum of voices covered the subtle music being piped in from speakers set around the area. Yet, despite the noise level, the babble died as the classic tune, strummed at countless ceremonies, the 'Wedding March' began to play. At the signal, everyone's attention, most especially Leo's, became riveted at the far end of the field.

First came the flower girls, pretty little lasses in summery frocks, skipping down the aisle, tossing handfuls of petals and, in one case, the basket when it was empty.

Next came the bridesmaids, Luna, strutting in her gown and heels, a challenging dare in her eyes that begged someone to make a remark about the girly getup she was forced to wear. Next came Reba and Zena, giggling and prancing, loving the attention.

This time, Leo wasn't thrown by Teena's appearance, nor was he fooled. How could he have mistaken her for his Vex? While similar outwardly, Meena's twin lacked the same confident grin, and the way she moved, with a delicate grace, did not resemble his bold woman at all. How unlike they seemed.

Until Teena tripped, flailed her arms, and took out part of a row before she could recover!

Yup, they were sisters all right.

With a heavy sigh, and pink cheeks, Teena managed to walk the rest of the red carpet, high heels in hand—one of which seemed short a heel.

With all the wedding party more or less safely arrived, there was only one person of import left. However, she didn't walk alone.

Despite his qualms, which Leo heard over the keg they'd shared the previous night, Peter appeared ready to give his daughter away. Ready, though, didn't mean he looked happy about it.

The seams of the suit his soon-to-be father-in-law wore strained, the rented tux not the best fit, but Leo doubted that was why he looked less than pleased. Leo figured there were two reasons for Peter's grumpy countenance. The first was the fact that he had to give his little girl away. The second probably had to do with the snickers and the repetition of a certain rumor, "I hear he lost an arm-wrestling bet and had to wear a tie."

For those curious, Leo had won that wager, and thus did his new father-in-law wear the, "gods-damned-noose" around his neck.

However, who cared about that sore loser when upon his arm rested a vision of beauty.

Meena's long hair tumbled in golden waves over her shoulders, the ends curled into fat ringlets that tickled her cleavage. At her temples, ivory combs swept the sides up and away, revealing the creamy line of her neck.

The strapless gown made her appear as a goddess. The bust, tight and low cut, displayed her fantastic breasts so well that Leo found himself growling. He didn't like the appreciative eyes in the crowd. Yet, at the same time, he felt a certain pride. His bride was beautiful, and it was only right she be admired.

From her impressive breasts, the gown cinched in before flaring out. The filmy white fabric of the skirt billowed as she walked. He noted she wore flats. Reba's suggestion so she wouldn't get a heel stuck. Her gown didn't quite touch the ground. Zena's idea to ensure she wouldn't trip on the hem.

They'd taken all kinds of precautions to ensure her the smoothest chance of success.

She might lack the feline grace of other ladies. She might have stumbled a time or two and been kept upright only by the smooth actions of her father, but dammit, in his eyes, she was the daintiest, most beautiful sight he'd ever seen.

And she is mine.

Her eyes met his, bright, shining, and filled with utmost happiness. Her smile conveyed that same joy, and he couldn't help but return it.

Even Peter couldn't dim his happiness. As he transferred Meena's hand to Leo, Peter bent his head and in a not-so-quiet whisper said, "Son, if you hurt her, I will eviscerate you. Slowly. Welcome to the family."

Such a heart-warming message. Then again, it went well with the one his new mother-in-law gave him once the ceremony was over and Meena was off giggling with the lionesses and telling them all to call her Mrs.

"Leo, darling, you seem like a nice boy, so I'm sure it goes without saying that if you hurt my daughter I will have you disappear, without a trace."

For some reason he asked, "How?"

And Meena's prim and proper mother gave him a smile, a smile to make any big man tremble as she said, "Have you heard about my prize-winning red roses?"

But that frightening fact came after the ceremony. In the here and now, Leo clung to Meena's hand and stared into her eyes as the priest recited the shifter version of a wedding. It contained most of the standard phrases.

"We are gathered here today to join this pair…"

Leo quite honestly tuned most of it out, too intent on the electrical crackle between him and Meena. He also concentrated on not passing out. No longer would he mock those AFV videos where the grooms went over with a crash. He could understand now why so many fainted. The tension of being in front of so many people, making such a deep commitment, all of it was enough to make even the biggest man tremble.

And then it was almost over.

The priest, as was customary, had to say, "If there is anyone here with a reason why these two beings should not become one in the eyes of the pride, then speak now or forever hold your peace."

Leo shot a glare at Dmitri, who sat at the back, but it wasn't he who stood.

With a clearing of his throat, Peter shot to his feet. He only managed to utter an "I—" before Meena's mom literally tackled him. She hit him around the knees and sent him tumbling to the grass. Even if she whispered it, in the stunned silence everyone heard her, "Zip it! My lovely daughter is having a white wedding. In a proper dress! Don't you dare ruin this for me."

And then Meena's mom plastered her husband lips with a kiss while waving at them in a get-this-done-and-quick gesture.

A pair of I do's, and then it was time to kiss his bride.

His wife.

Mine.

Paying no mind to the cheering, Leo bent his head. He had only one focus, the soft lips parted beneath his.

Drawing his wife into his arms, he hugged her to him and thoroughly explored her mouth. She explored him right back, her tongue weaving its way in and dancing along his.

Someone tapped him on the shoulder, and he growled.

Someone cleared their throat beside them, and she growled.

Voices spoke. People laughed, and it became more and more evident that they couldn't kiss forever. At least not out here. Neither could they immediately escape. Dammit.

No sooner had their lips separated than they both found themselves swept away in a tide of well wishes. Leo suffered the pounding on his back by the men, as well as the commiserations from a few on getting shackled.

Poor Meena was surrounded by a gaggle of her own.

Their eyes caught over the heads of the crowd but only for a moment before their attention was stolen.

While his patience frayed, in the end, it was Meena who snapped first.

Whether it was the fact a woman touched him, hanging on to his arm, gushing at how beautiful the wedding was, or the fact that Meena couldn't handle the frustration of the last few days, it didn't matter.

With a snarled, "Get your hands off my husband!" Meena sliced through the crowd, skirts hiked. She leaped the last few feet and soared through the air to tackle the lioness at his side, who, as it turned out, was Loni's cousin.

But at the time, all he knew was his new wife was in full-on jealous mode and determined to scalp a wedding guest.

As omega, Leo should have jumped in to calm the hot tempers—and stop the hair pulling. At the very least, he should have definitely pried Meena off the lioness before she got blood on her white dress.

But...

Well...

He kind of liked it. While Leo had dated his fair share of women, he'd never had one show such a possessive side before. Definitely never had one go after a girl for daring to flirt with him. He didn't know what it said about him, the fact that he enjoyed her jealous outburst.

Feeling kind of smug about it, he took a moment to bask.

Hers.

Yes, he was hers, and she was his, at least on paper. Perhaps it was time to complete the bond and truly mate so that everyone would know they belonged to each other. Time to claim each other.

First, though, he needed to pry her off the other woman before she literally spilled blood.

Winding an arm around her middle, he lifted Meena, even as she continued to snarl at the woman on the ground. "Touch my man again and I will rip that hand from you and slap you with it!"

Ah, the romantic words of a woman in lust.

Tossing Meena over his shoulder, he ignored the amused glances of the crowd as he carted her away from the party.

"I wasn't done, Pookie," she grumbled.

"I've got better plans for that energy," was his reply.

And yes, she announced to all that, "Leo's finally going to debauch me." She wasn't the only one fist pumping. The other ladies in the pride were cheering too while Leo fought not to blush, and poor Peter, he made a beeline for the bar.

However, embarrassment wasn't enough to stop him.

Reaching the door to their room, he almost laughed at the sign haphazardly hung saying 'Do Not Disturb' and scrawled underneath in red lipstick, 'Or Die'.

He couldn't agree more. The time had come for him to claim the woman who consumed him and beware the idiot who got in his way.

He'd no sooner slammed the door shut with his foot than she was sliding off his shoulder. Her arms wound around his neck as she plastered her lips against his. How yummy she tasted. The electrical awareness he felt only with her arced between them, fueling the simmering desire.

His lips slanted over hers, teasing and nibbling, claiming and branding that mouth for his own. She swallowed his groan as she opened her mouth and slid her tongue along his, teasing and taunting.

Instinct pulsed within him, pushing him to claim her, to mark her. Now.

Such impatience. Such need.

He let his hands rove her body, skimming over the silky fabric hiding her curves.

"Have I told you yet how beautiful you look?" he murmured against her skin as he let his lips trail down the smooth column of her neck.

"I can tell," she replied, her hand cupping his erection.

Her brazen nature delighted him. As did her squeeze of his cock.

"My English teacher always said to show, not tell." he said as he walked her backward toward the bed. He lay her down upon it, still clothed.

"Shouldn't I strip first?" she asked. Her hair spilled across the pillow in a golden puddle, and her lips, swollen from kisses, begged him for more.

He shook his head, "Oh no you don't. From the moment I saw you, I've fantasized about lifting that skirt and spreading it around to frame you when I take you."

"You had dirty thoughts during the ceremony?"

He couldn't help a naughty grin, to which she replied with a throaty laugh, "Oh, Pookie. You are so utterly wicked. And sly. I love how you can seem so serious and yet harbor such naughty thoughts."

"If you think that's awesome, then wait until I act them out."

With what he hoped was a diabolical arch of his brow, Leo shed his jacket and loosened his tie before he sank to his knees on the bed. Her bare feet—shoeless since she'd kicked off her flats before her wild dash—peeked from the hem of her dress. Under the filmy layers, he let his hand inch up her calf, higher still, his arm disappearing under the skirt. No seeing, only touch alone, which made it the more exciting as his fingertips brushed her thighs.

She sucked in a breath, her eyelids heavy as she watched him. He tickled the tips of his fingers higher and couldn't help but groan as he encountered the bareness of her mound. And he meant bare. Shaven and not even covered by a scrap of fabric.

"You married me wearing no panties?" He practically groaned it.

"Just in case we needed to go somewhere for a quickie," she admitted before sucking in a breath as he ran a knuckle over the moist lips of her sex.

"It's a good thing you didn't tell me beforehand."

"Or?"

"We might not have made it through the ceremony."

"You might not live the next few minutes if you don't stop talking and do something."

"Impatient, Vex?"

"Try horny," she grumbled. Rolling to her knees, she grabbed his face and kissed him. Kissed him hard as she pushed against him, tumbling him to his back.

Despite his clothes, she straddled him, her hands clutching the linen at his shoulders while she aggressively chewed at his lips. Unbridled passion that could no longer wait.

With her skirts hiked around her in a fluffy cloud and her cleft pressed against his groin, despite his pants separating them, he couldn't miss the radiating heat.

Her rocking against him as they kissed proved the height of torture. He wanted so badly to sink into her. Instead, his hands busied themselves, cupping her full cheeks, an ass he loved to massage and squeeze. He loved even more the soft sounds she made against his mouth. Pressed tight to him, her splendid breasts, squashed against his chest, their cushion reminded him how much he enjoyed them.

I must touch. Taste.

It became an imperative need. He manhandled her, bringing her body forward over him so that her bosom hung over his mouth. They practically spilled from the square neckline, so it took only a little manipulation to have them heave out. He allowed her to sit back down on his chest but only so he could free his hands to cup those gorgeous mounds.

Palming her heavy breasts, he admired them as he brushed a thumb over her nipple. Instantly, it shriveled into a tight bud. He drew her forward so that her breasts hung over his mouth. He licked the tip of one, and a shudder rocked her body.

Angling his mouth, he brought himself close enough to truly play with those pebbled delights. As his mouth latched onto one protruding nipple, he allowed his fingers to tug and twist the other.

He could gauge her enjoyment via her cries of pleasure, by how she arched, pressing her plump breast against his mouth, encouraging him to take more.

So he did. He inhaled the tip into his mouth, sucking and biting. With every gasp she emitted, with every soft mewl and quiver in her body, the tension within him built.

So responsive to his touch. So…gone from his face.

He almost roared when she took them away. But not too far. Oh hell, what was she planning?

His bride knelt between his legs, her dress pulled down under her breasts, the skin of them flushed. Her skirt billowed out around her when she crouched, but of more interest to his avid gaze was what she did.

Nimble fingers undid the buttons to his shirt and spread it, baring his chest. She raked nails down the flesh, drawing a shiver from him and then a shudder as her hands didn't stop at the waistband to his trousers.

A slip of the button, a whir as a zipper descended and she gasped as she beheld him.

"You went commando to our wedding?"

Before he could reply, she did with an "awesome" that ended up somewhat garbled as she drew him into her mouth.

At that point, he just about came. And then she pressed her breasts around him as she sucked the tip. Covered him in soft flesh and then slid his shaft back and forth while keeping a latch.

Yeah. He was a goner.

CHAPTER TWENTY-FOUR

Leo's essence spurted hotly, and she captured every drop. He bellowed her name as he came, such a lovely sound.

Such a wonderful man.

My man.

Her mate who retained a certain hardness even though he came. She sucked at him for a moment until he growled, "My turn."

His turn? How did he figure that? She'd just made him climax.

Except by his turn, he really meant hers.

"Get on your back," he demanded.

Instead, she rolled to her knees and peered over her shoulder at him. "You're not the only one with a fantasy," she observed.

"Best. Wedding. Present. Ever." Leo apparently liked where this was headed. His hand ran over the curve of her ass then down until he found the fluffy edge of her skirt. Slowly, he pulled the fabric up and away from her thighs and buttocks.

Still watching him over her shoulder, she noted his cock already bobbing again. He drew closer, closer. She shivered, but he surprised her. Instead of sinking into her, he bent over and his tongue lapped at her sex.

Dear heaven.

Back and forth he licked, the lithe motion exciting. The flick of his tongue on her clitoris breathtaking. The plunge of two fingers into her channel moan worthy.

Slowly, he pleasured her, each thrust of his digits and swipe of his tongue building her bliss, building into a tower that threatened to topple.

"Now, please," she practically sobbed.

She didn't have to beg twice. He shuffled on the bed until he knelt directly behind her, the tip of his cock nudging her wet slit. He eased the head in slowly.

Too slowly.

She rammed back against him, echoing his cried, "Ah," at the suddenness.

But oh, the pleasure.

Finally, he was in her. Stretching her. He also moved within her, short, grinding thrusts that pressed the swollen head of him against her most sensitive spot.

Over and over. Push. Grind. Squeeze. *Oh.*

The joining was so perfect, so intense, it took only the smallest pinch of his teeth on her skin, just hard enough to break skin, for her to come apart.

Awareness slammed into her as he laid his claim on her, as he truly made her his mate, not just in the eyes of human law but in primal law as well.

They both let loose a wild roar as their ecstasy hit, a wave like no other.

As her climax shuddered through her, she cried, "Harder. Harder."

And he gave it to her. Pounded her fast, hard, fully. Against her ass, he slapped, his body a perfect fit for her, a body that could handle her and her passion.

How hot his cream as it bathed her womb. How voice-stealing her own orgasm as number two wrung her hoarse.

As their heart rates slowed, their bodies cooled, and they came down from their high, Leo spooned her. He collapsed to his side and drew her against him, fitting her against his body. Holding her.

It was wonderful. Perfect.

Crack!

So of course the bed chose that moment to break on one side and tilt them toward the floor.

"Damn you, universe," she shouted, shaking a fist.

And what did Leo do at this perfect example of a catastrophe?

He laughed while she rawred.

EPILOGUE

"Morning, Vex." Leo nuzzled the top of her head.

"It is the bestest morning ever, Pookie." It totally was. Just over a week since their wedding, and she could say, with certainty, she got happier every day.

As Meena stretched, her movement atop Leo roused her big and burly mate, and by roused, she meant *roused*. It had become part of their morning routine. They now had many routines, such as her new sleeping spot.

What a novelty. Snoozing atop another person without needing to call an ambulance or find a Weight Watchers pamphlet taped to the fridge.

The first time she slid off him before she fell asleep, he'd yanked her right back on with a growled, "Don't you dare move."

"Even I can't get into too much trouble when I sleep," she'd teased, resting her head on his chest but perfectly content to return to her snuggly spot.

"Get into as much trouble as you like, Vex, so long as you keep that luscious body right here where it belongs.

You're a hell of a lot warmer and cuddlier than any blanket."

Yeah, that sweet compliment got him some nookie. Leo was always doing and saying the nicest things, so he got nookie quite often actually.

Leo proved more amazing than she could have ever hoped for. Patient despite the fact mishaps followed her. Intelligent and capable of keeping her mind entertained. Sexy and giving when it came to loving in the bedroom. And possessed of a sense of humor, which was important, given how they'd broken their fourth bed last night.

Eyeballing the broken welds on the headboard of the brass bed, she remarked, "Who do you think won the bet this time?" Because, after the first two bed mishaps, a betting pool started.

"I won," Leo purred as he flipped her onto her back.

"You mean you wagered on us breaking the bed?"

"Hell yeah I did. But I won more than that. I totally scored when it came to finding you."

"Don't you mean I found you? I mean, after all, it was my Frisbee that smacked you in the head."

"A Frisbee I could have caught."

"You never saw—" He shook his head. She giggled. "Pookie, you sly devil, do you mean you purposely let yourself get smacked by it just to meet me? But if that's the case, then why play hard to get?"

"Because you scared me but that was before I realized you were exactly what I needed. I love you, Vex."

"Pookie!" she squealed as she plastered him with smooches. "I love you too, so much that I am totally going to forget about the fact that Reba and Zena have a ticket for me to go to Russia and rescue my sister."

"And miss out on a chance at a honeymoon? Did I forget to mention I'm going too? What do you say we go pay a tiger a visit?"

"Aren't you afraid I might start a war?"

"I'd be more surprised if you didn't. Now enough talking, Vex. It's time for our morning nookie."

And while they couldn't break the bed any further, the condo below them did complain about cracking plaster.

Rawr!

"SAY I DO."

"Hunh?" Eyes closed, and the lids too heavy to lift, her mouth a fuzzy peach in need of water, Teena's mind struggled to wake from the most molasses sleep ever.

"Say I do," hissed an accented voice for a second time.

"I do?" What did she do? Last she recalled, she was partying and drinking at her sister's wedding, and letting a certain Russian tiger flirt with her. Then…

Nothing.

Giving her cobwebbed brain a mental shake, she pried her eyes open in time to see Dmitri's handsome face hovering close to hers and hear the words, "I now pronounce you man and wife. You may kiss the bride."

What?!

NOT THE END!

Because now we have to go on a humorous ride with, A Tiger's Bride.

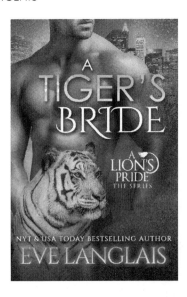

More books in A Lion's Pride, a USA Today Bestselling series:

Be sure to visit www.EveLanglais for more books with furry heroes, or sign up for the Eve Langlais newsletter for notification about new stories or specials.

Made in the USA
Columbia, SC
06 November 2024

45824243R00109